THE CONJUROR'S BOX

THE
CONJUROR'S
BOX

Ann Lawrence

ILLUSTRATED BY
BRIAN ALLDRIDGE

KESTREL BOOKS

KESTREL BOOKS
Published by Penguin Books Ltd
Harmondsworth, Middlesex, England

Text Copyright © 1974 by Ann Lawrence
Illustrations Copyright © 1974 by Penguin Books Ltd

First published 1974

ISBN 0 7226 6806 6

Printed in Great Britain by
Western Printing Services Ltd, Bristol

*To Grandfather Brady
who first introduced me to
Snowy and the striped mouse*

CONTENTS

1

HEY DIDDLE DIDDLE

MARTIN LOVELL sprawled across the table aimlessly pushing the many unidentifiable pieces of his jigsaw puzzle around the few which he had managed to fit together. He yawned hugely.

'Is it still raining?' he said without looking up.

His sister Lucy, who was sitting on the window seat with a pad of drawing paper on her knee, said:

'Mmm,' and continued to chew her pencil and stare out of the window at the dripping garden.

Great-Aunt Bea had suggested that they should spend the last week-end of the Easter holidays with her in London.

'It'll stop you thinking about the awfulness of having to go back to school,' she had said. 'We'll go to the theatre on Saturday afternoon, and on Sunday I'll take you to a toy fair. How does that sound?'

It had sounded like a very good idea. Aunt Bea had given them lunch in a restaurant which they thought was no end smart, *and* she had allowed them to have whatever they chose, instead of insisting that everything they liked would make them sick. That was a treat in itself, but then they had gone to see *A Midsummer Night's Dream*, and because it was raining when they came out of the theatre, they had come back to Aunt Bea's flat in a taxi. It was all very satisfactory.

After that, however, the day had sagged into anti-climax. Aunt Bea had suddenly remembered that she had to see someone, and had gone out leaving the children to amuse themselves for an hour.

'There's a new jigsaw and plenty of paper and pencils,' she had said as she whisked out.

But the rain seemed to have dampened their spirits and their excitement had definitely gone off the boil.

Silence descended on the flat. The afternoon was so overcast now that the light was already failing and the air seemed to be thick with dusk, muffling the ticking of the clock and the tiny crackling, clinking noises from the fire. The clock, clicking and whirring as it prepared to strike, sounded almost too tired to make the effort. Lucy felt slightly uneasy. More for the sake of breaking the silence than because she expected Martin to be interested she said:

'I'm going to draw Puck muddling up the people.'

But Martin only grunted and the silence ignored her. She carefully wrote the title of her picture at the top of the page, and then leaned against the window, staring down into the garden. It was so wet out there that it was like looking into an aquarium, and she wondered what would have happened to all those people in a wood near Athens if it had rained.

Martin idly kicked the nearest table leg and gazed around vacantly. The firelight jumped round the walls, and as he watched it flickering on the crockery and glasses on the dresser, he thought that the pictures on the painted plates seemed to move as the light caught them, while the glasses winked and twinkled at him. The dancing light drew his attention to something on the middle shelf, something he had never seen before: a small green jug with a little white china cat climbing up the side to serve as a handle.

The cat's front paws rested on the rim of the jug, and it looked as if it had just raised its head to look over. Every time the firelight gleamed on the jug the cat seemed to lean forward a little, and the longer Martin watched it in the tricky light, the more it seemed to him that the cat really was pulling itself further up the side, until he was sure he had seen it put its head right into the jug.

A moment later the tiny cat turned its head to look straight at him and winked.

'Lu,' Martin said uneasily, staring at the white cat as it slipped off the jug, yawned and stretched luxuriously.

Lucy turned from the window and followed his gaze just in time to see the cat jump from the shelf to the edge of the dresser, where it stopped and looked long and thoughtfully at each child in turn. Then it dropped to the floor, strolled to the hearthrug and settled itself down, tucking in its front paws and blinking contentedly at the fire.

Still the children stared. The cat was no longer so very small – indeed it was now quite a large and imposing animal: smooth and silky coated, with a curly, smiling mouth and very bright blue eyes.

'Hasn't your mother ever told you it's rude to stare?' said the cat at last, still gazing into the fire.

Martin and Lucy looked at each other in consternation, and then hastily back at the cat, which was looking over its shoulder and plainly laughing at them.

'Beg your pardon,' Martin mumbled and Lucy nodded mutely.

'Well,' said the cat after another pause, 'haven't you anything else to say for yourselves? No questions? Don't tell me this sort of thing happens every afternoon.'

Lucy slid off the window seat and cleared her throat awkwardly.

'Are you . . . er . . . what . . . ?' she began, '. . . who . . . ?'

'Oh come now! No ceremony please!' said the cat sarcastically. 'You may call me Snowy, as your great-great-grandfather did when I first went with him as ship's cat on the clipper *Halcyon*.' He bowed graciously to them and Lucy bobbed an uncertain curtsy in return.

'You knew our great-great-grandfather?' Whether the cat thought it rude or not Martin could not help staring.

'That is correct,' said Snowy. 'It was a very convenient arrangement – I travelled a good deal in those days, and I always liked
the sea. I have been acquainted with five generations of your
family actually (including yourselves – I think we can call
ourselves acquainted now, can't we?), though you'd hardly think

it to see the way your great-aunt greeted me the other day. The human memory for anything of the slightest importance apparently ceases to function after the age of thirteen. And it's not all that reliable before then.'

The white cat sniffed and licked his shoulder briefly.

'Five generations! Then you must be more than a hundred years old!' Martin exclaimed. 'You're an antique!'

Snowy's ears flattened and his claws flexed.

'As it happens I am considerably more than a hundred years old,' he said coldly, 'but "antique" is not a word I should choose to apply to myself. However, if you were referring to that vulgar piece of china, that is rather less than a hundred years old.'

Martin, who had intended the remark to be complimentary, wilted a little, and Lucy said hastily:

'So you weren't always part of that jug?'

'Do I look as if an All-Wise Providence intended me for a jug handle?' the cat demanded.

'Oh dear, was it an accident?' Lucy quavered. She thought the question sounded silly even as she said it, but the cat seemed to make everything they said sound silly.

'Very far from it. Nothing was ever more deliberate,' said Snowy bitterly.

He brooded sombrely at the fire, while the children stood in silence, reluctant to provoke his sarcasm again. Eventually he looked up at them.

'Well, don't you want to know what happened?' he said. 'What a dull lot you are! Or don't you think you need to be told any more about it – seeing that you've known the bones of the story most of your lives?' A tantalizing smile crept into the corners of his mouth and he looked at them wickedly.

The children looked at each other and shook their heads.

'I don't think . . .' Lucy began.

'That's just the trouble,' said the cat unfairly. 'No human being ever does until it's too late, and that's why I shall never be out of a job. But if you sit down and listen for a few minutes, I can save you the trouble of thinking.'

The children sat down on the hearthrug with the white cat, who stared into the fire again. It was so long before he spoke again that Martin began to think he had forgotten about them, and then, very softly, he said:

'Hey diddle diddle
The cat . . .'

'Was that *you*?' Martin whispered. 'The cat and the fiddle?'

Snowy grinned at the fire.

'There was a fiddle, some ill-disciplined cutlery and a few other things that behaved quite disgracefully, to be sure.' His grin faded and he shifted discontentedly. 'And the upshot of it all as far as I was concerned was that I got stuck to that disgusting utensil.' He glared at the children. 'I must say, the knowledge that one's misfortune is bandied about every nursery in the country is one of the most humiliating aspects of the whole humiliating affair,' he added bitterly, as if they were personally responsible for the situation.

'It just goes to show,' he went on, 'that even the most astute mind may be deceived. So *you'd* better look out.'

'Why?' said Martin. 'What's going to happen?'

'Why?' repeated the cat; the hair rose along his back and his voice sank into a growl. 'Because what's going to happen is that this time we are really going to *fix* Her, and we shan't get far with that if you two get yourselves turned into book-ends, shall we?' He spat out the last words and glowered at Martin balefully.

'*Who* is going to be fixed, and why should we get turned into anything?' Lucy asked desperately, thinking that she would scream in a minute if the aggravating animal did not tell them what he was talking about.

Snowy composed himself and shook his head reproachfully.

'Look, we are starting at quite the wrong end of the story,' he said patiently, as if this were all the children's fault. 'We must go back a bit – to the year 1890 or thereabouts. The *whole* story goes back a lot further, but that's where we'll start – in the year when your great-great-grandfather, Captain Lovell of the *Halcyon*, found a small green statue of a woman in a bazaar in Bombay, and bought it for his wife.

'She liked that sort of thing, you see: she had a glass-fronted cupboard full of bits and pieces – Chinese ivories, a little lady and gentleman made of porcelain and quite a lot of silver. The famous dish and spoon were part of her silver collection – the dish was broad and shallow and the spoon was a long-handled object with a flat, leaf-shaped bowl – not a lot of use for spooning I'd say. The Captain had found *them* on his travels too, though heaven knows where. The rest of the silver was very English, Georgian and aristocratic – you know, a bit bulgy and overdecorated. If anything in the cupboard was going to behave eccentrically, you would have thought it would have been that lot, but then, you never really know how anything will react in a crisis, and the quietest are usually the ones who surprise you.'

'What about the cow?' Lucy asked.

Snowy sniggered.

'That was Daisy,' he said. 'She was a cream jug in the shape of a cow, with flowers painted on her sides. She really was the silliest object I've ever come across, I can tell you.'

'And the little dog – was he real?' asked Martin.

'What do you mean by "real"?' Snowy demanded. 'Are you suggesting that the other things *weren't* real? He was a low bandy-legged animal, said to be a variety of dachshund and called Pickle – though I don't know if that referred to his confused ancestry or his talent for trouble. Would you call that real?'

'I meant alive,' Martin said. 'Not just a *thing*.'

'You'd be surprised to know how alive the creatures you refer to as "just things" are,' Snowy said. 'It varies of course – you find that furniture is pretty sluggish as a rule, while at the other end of the scale things like toys are usually bursting with vitality.

'*Things* are like electric batteries you see – storage cells – only instead of storing electricity, they store life, imagination, enjoyment. People put all sorts of ideas and feeling into the Things they make and live with, and when they're feeling low, they draw on their Things for a boost. So it stands to reason that the livelier people are the livelier the Things around them will be. The Things in Captain Lovell's house were particularly lively, because he had three energetic and imaginative children.

'But all that started to change the moment your great-great-grandmother stood her Green Lady on top of the glass-fronted cupboard in the drawing room.

'I was away at the time on my own, but I felt the difference in the house the moment I came back – it had gone all cold and mean. Every single Thing seemed to be exhausted, and it wasn't the family that had been drawing off energy, because they were in a pretty bad way themselves: the children were sulky, their mother said she was suffering from nerves (a woman who'd never known she had a nerve in her body before that!), and the cook was giving notice twice a week. The Captain had gone back to sea believing that his family had gone completely mad, poor man.

'Pickle told me all about it (even he looked only half the dog he used to be) and I was disturbed. It was more than just uncomfortable – it was downright sinister. Perfectly normal families don't suddenly start having sulks and vapours for no reason. I started to look around for anything that was new since I had last been there, and I found two newcomers: the Green Lady and a bronze statue of an old man, very tall and thin and fantastical, playing the queerest fiddle you ever saw – it was a longhandled shovel that he bowed with a pair of tongs. Right, I thought, it's one of you.

'At first I thought it must be the Fiddler, because he was the only Thing in the house that seemed to be unaffected by the depressing atmosphere – *he* was full of beans whereas the Green

Lady just stood on top of the cupboard, completely still and silent. But the Fiddler stood on a little table in the hall, and I found that the centre of the unpleasantness was in the drawing room. It had to be the Lady. Once you'd noticed it, it was like a physical sensation – a sort of cold pins and needles that grew stronger as you approached her.

'I went up to the cupboard and looked at her. I could see that she was looking at *me*, so I said: "What are you doing?" She said: "What is that to you, cat?" and closed her eyes, but I felt her mind running over me like cold fingers. What she found puzzled her, I could tell that, she couldn't work it out and in the end she said: "Go away cat, you do not concern me." Oh, I thought, do I not indeed?

'It was towards the end of October and it was time I went about my business – I'd hung around longer than I'd intended already – but I couldn't leave until I'd sorted this Lady character out. She'd gradually brought the whole household under some noxious spell, that was obvious, but how to break it? I went looking for Pickle to ask him what he made of it; he'd been there all the time so he might have some ideas. I found him in the hall trying to slide on the mats, but they wouldn't co-operate.

' "What we need is a bit of Fun," he said mournfully. "We haven't had any Fun for ages." He was very much in favour of Fun, was that young dog. Then there came a little twiddle of music, and we looked up to find that the Fiddler was listening to us. "How about a party?" he said. "A farewell party before Snowy goes away again – a Hallowe'en party." He played a few bars of a weird, compelling waltz and said: "I'll provide the music." '

Snowy stared at the fire in silence for a while.

'I should have known then – all the hairs stirred on my back – I should have guessed . . . We could have managed things so much better. . . But I didn't so we couldn't.'

He returned briskly to his story from whatever thought had distracted him.

'At first the response to the idea of a party was very poor: all the Things were so apathetic by that time that you could hardly make them understand. But some of the toys in the nursery at the very top of the house still had a bit of go in them, and once they had roused themselves the children cheered up, and that made a world of difference.

'The party was a great success. Everything that could do so crowded into the drawing room – people out of books and pictures as well as the toys and ornaments and things like that. The Green Lady stood aloof from our low revel, but it seemed to me that she was particularly interested in a couple of my particular friends, whom she probably had not seen until then: they were a boggart who lived in the kitchen inglenook, and a dryad who usually hung about a willow tree in the garden but always found some excuse for spending most of the winter indoors.

'The Fiddler played for our dances, and that instrument of his produced music that drew your feet after it before you knew what was happening . . . that should have made me think. . .

'Towards midnight someone touched me on the shoulder and I found the Fiddler standing beside me. He offered me his fiddle and said: "Come on Snowy, you must know a tune or two worth hearing." There was a sly smile on his face, and he dropped half a wink towards the Green Lady, as if to say: "See if *you* can't make her sit up."

'The moment I took that fiddle in my paws, I knew that it was something even stranger than it looked, for it near enough played itself. It played my thoughts, and since at that moment I was thinking how good it would be to get down to the sea again, all the tunes it played were shanties and hornpipes: tunes for working to and tunes to dance to when the work was done. The whole company gathered round singing and clapping. *I* would have stopped presently, but the fiddle would not. The old man nodded and smiled still, and the fiddle went on – playing tunes I'd never heard before, except in dreams perhaps, for now it made music of the magic of the sea that draws even those who know it at its worst – especially them maybe. It played brisk blue and white mornings in the Channel and the mountainous seas of the Atlantic, boiling storms off Cape Horn and soft nights in the tropics. There was the creak of timbers and wind in the rigging in every note: it sang the lure of every foreign port from Archangel to Rio. The singing, clapping group around me broke up and whirled away in a fantastic dance. The music ran high and swift, almost out of hearing. . .

'At the first stroke of midnight all the windows flew open with a bang and everyone stopped dancing, but the fiddle did not stop playing. On the second stroke, Daisy careered across the room mooing crazily, collided with a vase of flowers on the window sill, and disappeared into the night with a couple of roses tangled round her horns. On the third stroke the full moon which hung low in the sky turned bright blue before our eyes, and we saw the tiny silhouette of Daisy sailing over it. On the fourth stroke Pickle started to yap with laughter, bouncing up and down on all four feet, while everyone stared stupidly from the window to him and back to the window again, until he fell over and lay on his back wriggling and kicking and still laughing. Then they all started laughing excitedly, but the fiddle fretted on and I could not stop it. Everyone surged towards the windows and hovered a moment. The clock struck again and the foreign dish and spoon, which had never before done anything to indicate that there was a spark of life in them, skimmed lightly out into the garden. The rest of the silver bounded after them, hooting and tally-hoing gallantly, followed by the toys and then everything else, until at the twelfth stroke the room was empty except for the Fiddler, Pickle, the Green Lady and myself while the rest of the party streamed across the garden in the blue moonlight. At last the fiddle stopped and in the silence the clock struck once more.

'As my wits began to return to me I realized that the Lady was staring at me with the coldest, most baleful expression I have ever seen. The old man took back his wicked fiddle, tucked it under his chin and played a tiny rising flourish which I had heard before – but a very long time before. He bowed low to the Lady still smiling gently, and turned to the nearest window. As he stepped out everything that I ought to have noticed the moment I set eyes on him snapped into place and I started after him, but something pulled me up.

'In the surprise of recognizing the Fiddler, I had completely forgotten the Lady and so I was off my guard. I made no attempt to defend myself, because it was not until I felt myself stiffening under her cold, green gaze that I realized there was any danger. By then it was too late, and I found myself stuck to a small green jug.

'Pickle tried to roll under the sofa, hoping she had forgotten him, but he was out of luck. He looked even odder in china than he had as a living animal – white, with a Dutch landscape in blue on both sides.'

Lucy sighed deeply.

'Poor Pickle,' she said. 'And poor Snowy. Is it wearing off now?'

'In fact it never was as strong a spell as she thought,' Snowy said calmly. 'Less effective because she didn't know *exactly* what I was, and we appeared to have weakened her anyway by waking up the Things, so I recovered a certain amount of mobility quite soon. However, I don't think it can ever "wear off" as you say. It will have to be broken – and she's the only one who knows how it can be done.'

'What about all the Things that ran away?' Martin asked. 'What did the people in the house think about it?'

'What could they think?' said Snowy. 'The house was in an uproar for days. Everyone declared that there'd been a burglary – but it was the silliest burglary ever! A cat and a dog had disappeared, being replaced with china substitutes; the Green Lady, who was certainly valuable, had been left where she stood, but the toys from the nursery had been taken; books had been pulled out of bookcases and pictures had been dragged from the walls, but most of them had been dropped in the garden and along the lane beyond. In fact half the contents of the house had been spread all over the surrounding countryside.

'Most of the runaways were recovered within a mile of home. The Chinese ivories had apparently headed due east to start with, but had lost their way and were found in a cottage garden two fields away. The silver was discovered scattered round a clearing in a near-by wood, a little battered and thoroughly debauched – *they* obviously only wanted a night out. The toys, on the other hand, must have had serious intentions of seeing the world, for it was a week before they were found in company with a number of books on foreign travel, camping in a hedge alongside the road to the coast.

'The dish and the spoon were never seen again, and neither was Daisy. I eventually caught up with the Fiddler, but by that time he had taken a new disguise, so to all intents and purposes he was never seen again either.'

'Who *was* the Fiddler?' Lucy asked.

'Who *was* the Fiddler indeed,' Snowy murmured. 'Let us say – he was someone I had known long ago – someone had I thought I should be bound to know again. But then, *he* might have expected to recognize me. . . We are in the same business, you see.'

The cat turned his bright blue stare on the children and smiled mysteriously.

'What about the Green Lady?' Martin demanded. 'Is it her we've got to fix? Who is she anyway? And why—?'

Snowy squeezed his eyes shut and hissed shortly.

'If only you would keep quiet, I could tell you everything in an orderly manner,' he said irritably. 'Where was I? Yes, well, we had checked the harm she had been doing to the Lovell household, but we lost the advantage of our success immediately. The Fiddler had gone, believing that everything would be all right after that, I was immobilized, and very shortly the Lady herself was sold. Your great-great-grandmother took against her in a big way – said she was unlucky and that all the trouble was due to her. She was right of course, but it made things difficult for me. I knew from what she had done to Pickle and myself that the Lady was a bit more than just a nuisance, but with my limited mobility it took me a long time to get in touch with the Fiddler again. When I did manage it, he told me all he knew about Madam, much of which I had guessed already.

'It appeared that she was originally one of those beings that humans in old times called gods – quite an important one too in her heyday and worshipped by many people. She had held the seasons in her hands, the increase of herds and the ripening of harvests. When the world changed and these beings lost most of their powers, she would not accept that her day was over, and she bitterly resented the new order. At first she fought it, then she sulked, and eventually she was forgotten. Within a few generations of men she had only one shrine left and one statue. It's true that the shrine had been sacred to her since the dawn of history and the statue was so ancient that people said it had fallen from the sky – but what a come-down! One country shrine and one little green statue! Then war came, the shrine was abandoned and the statue disappeared . . . to turn up years later in that Bombay bazaar.

' "You knew all this and yet you thought it was enough to slap her down and then leave her alone?" I said. He shrugged. "I knew she was malicious, but I didn't think she had the power to be dangerous any more," he said. "Well, she's found some way of regaining power," I said, "and there's no knowing what she'll do with it." "I think *I* know," he said. "She'll try to punish human-kind for rejecting her." He looked as if he were beginning to see how serious things were by that time.

'So we started to look for her. The trail was cold by then, and it was years before we picked it up. When we did we were not reassured. Everywhere she had been, she had done exactly the same thing as she had done in Captain Lovell's house – drawing the energy out of the Things humans live with to increase her own power. And as Things become more human when humans put life into them, so the humans became more Thingish as she drew that life into herself.

'First she had gone to work in a small way – draining each household she entered – then as she grew stronger she began to enlarge her operations. We soon realized that she had others working for her: playing the same trick all over the country and feeding her with power. She discovered that machinery could be useful to her – a great deal of human ingenuity goes into machines and they are very easy to "drain" it seems. If she could surround humans with lifeless, mechanical Things, she could draw off the power of their imaginations like water from a tap. And it was so easy once she started! Human beings are apparently ready to fall for any gadget put in front of them!'

The cat glanced at the children disdainfully.

'As we closed in on her, we began to see what she would do with this world if her plan succeeded,' he continued. 'She would reduce humans to the state of mechanical dolls – all their independence, imagination, creativity being sucked out of them to feed her power. Quite by chance we discovered that she had another plan too. . .' Snowy hesitated. . . 'I can't explain that now, but it would make us powerless against her, if she were ever able to put it into operation. We knew we had to stop her – and then suddenly she disappeared.

'That was in 1939. For a while we tried to keep watch for her, but like everyone else we had a lot on our minds about that time.'

'Did she cause the war?' Martin asked.

Snowy thought about the question for a minute. Then he said:

'No. I expect she would be pleased enough at the amount of human misery it caused, but she would not have been sufficiently powerful then to start it. Besides, that wouldn't be her way – war is wasteful, it squanders energy at a tremendous rate, and she wants to draw all energy into herself.

'And anyhow, as I said, she completely disappeared at the beginning of the war, and her power was definitely checked. When it was all over her agents reappeared, but there was no sign of her. Since she had been in London when we had last heard of her, we assumed at last – unwisely – that she must have been destroyed somehow in the Blitz, and we let the matter drop. Well,' the cat sounded a little defensive, 'she had been inactive for twenty years by that time. It was not *so* unreasonable. The Fiddler and I went our separate ways again. But I was naturally always on the look out for a way of ridding myself of my confounded china shackle, and so I still kept a feeler out for any information about our late adversary. I heard rumours from time to time, which was to be expected – what was not to be expected was the way they became more, rather than less frequent. At last I received information that convinced me that the Green Lady is still quite formidably alive, and ready to move again.

' I may have said enough by now to explain why I feel that she must be found and dealt with quickly.'

Snowy looked at the children as if he were assessing how much use they would be in the coming action. Lucy doubted whether they could be of any use at all.

'But what can *we* do?' she asked nervously.

'For one thing,' said Snowy rising and stretching, 'you are going to take me back to Dunsley when you go home on Monday. That's where the next round is due to be played unless I'm much mistaken. In the meantime, keep your eyes open and see if you can spot any signs of her work.'

Suddenly his ears pricked and he looked at the door.

The children heard the sound of the flat door opening, then

footsteps in the hallway. The door opened and Aunt Bea flicked on the light.

'Why ever are you sitting around in the dark?' she exclaimed. 'What a pair you are. Look, you haven't had a bit of tea, and I left it all ready for you. Fetch the teapot into the kitchen Lucy, and Martin can pull the fire together and toast those buns.'

They wondered why she said nothing about Snowy, but when they looked round for him, they found that he had vanished. The little white cat was clinging to the side of the jug on the dresser again as though he had never stirred.

2

THE GREEN LADY

MARTIN and Lucy did not discuss the amazing appearance of the white cat that night, and they had no time to do so in the turmoil of Aunt Bea's preparations next morning. She had intended to make an early start, but somehow it was mid morning before they were ready to set out.

'My life is like a meandering stream,' Aunt Bea complained. '(See if you can find the paper cups, dear.) It silts up with things to be done and before I know what's happening, it's completely changed its course. Poor Dorothy will be quite sure by now that I'm not coming.'

Her niece and nephew did not ask her what she was talking about, because they knew from long experience that Aunt Bea never managed to explain anything at the first attempt. Often indeed she never managed to explain some things at all. It was not unknown for her to assemble a group of people to do something, without at any time telling them clearly what it was she wanted them to do, and if someone ventured, very cautiously, to ask what it was all about, she would look at them in amazement and exasperation, saying, 'But I told you all about it!' So far, Martin and Lucy had discovered only that the toy fair was being held at Olympia. Aunt Bea was a great organizer but a very bad explainer.

However, if one listened very carefully to everything she said, it was possible to work out what was going on, and by following her round the flat as she distractedly filled thermos flasks and wrapped up food, the children gathered that her reason for going to Olympia that Sunday morning was not to show them a lot

26

of toys, but to help a friend of hers, who was one of the exhibitors, to set up her stand. They also learned that Mrs Marsh's toys were hand-made by people working in their own homes, that Aunt Bea had been helping her recently, and that she now felt very guilty about her failure to arrive in time to put in a full day's work on the stand.

They were about to leave the flat, and Aunt Bea was gloomily anticipating the difficulties they would have in finding any form of public transport on a Sunday morning, when she appeared to be struck suddenly by an inspiration.

'Wait!' she ordered and disappeared in the direction of the basement flat. In a few minutes she reappeared and waggled a car key triumphantly under the children's noses.

'We shan't be *so* late after all!' she said, leading them out of the house and round the corner.

She stopped by a low orange sports car, unlocked it and ordered the children into the back. Martin was impressed beyond words.

'There's this charming young man who's just moved in down-stairs,' she said as she pulled away from the kerb. 'He's a student I think. He's kind enough to lend me his car when he's not using it, and he comes up to me for dinner now and then in return. I wonder if he's one of your father's students? We must ask him.'

'I don't think Daddy likes his students very much,' Lucy said doubtfully, thinking that it was quite possible that they might feel the same about *him*. 'He says that having to teach them is the price he pays for doing the work that interests him.'

'And he wouldn't like one that had a car,' Martin added. 'He doesn't even like *our* car – he says it's a malevolent brute. And he *hates* other people's.'

Aunt Bea cornered like a racing driver and shook her head sadly.

'I don't understand that nephew of mine,' she said. 'I thought scientists were practical men.'

'That's what Granddad says when Daddy complains about the car,' Lucy told her. 'But he says he's a mathematician not a motor mechanic, and there's no reason why he should have anything to do with the innards of the car, and,' she took a deep breath, 'the internal combustion engine is a very crude concept anyway.'

'Is it begad!' exclaimed Aunt Bea. 'Well I don't care how crude your clever father thinks it is, I like this one.'

That was very plain. Aunt Bea had learnt to drive in days when there was much less traffic and much more room for an individual style of driving. Never having seen any reason for changing her habits, she still drove with relish and enthusiasm, scything through Kensington like a motorized Boadicea and compelling other road-users to rearrange themselves around her triumphant passage. Had he been able to see them at that moment, Dr Lovell would certainly have given up any hope of seeing his children alive again.

When they arrived at Olympia it turned out that Aunt Bea's anxiety had been groundless. Mrs Marsh had only just arrived herself, and they found her on her empty stand, a small birdlike person surrounded by unopened boxes, urging a younger woman and a man to look out for a white-haired lady with two children. When she saw them approaching through the confusion of wires and lights, planks and packing cases, she waved and called anxiously:

'Oh Bea! I was so worried . . . sure you must have given us up . . . it was the van . . . and then John . . . have you met my daughter and her husband? They're helping us. . . Are these Richard's children? How nice. . .'

With great presence of mind Aunt Bea avoided the need to explain that she too was late, and suggested that now they were all assembled they had better set to at once. Lucy and Martin were told that there was nothing they could do to help at the moment, and so they wandered off to look round the exhibition hall, protected by lapel badges which informed anyone who needed to know that they were representatives of Friendly Toys Ltd, but nobody had time even to notice them, let alone inquire who they were and why they were there. The whole vast building seemed to be in a state of desperate chaos, and the children picked their way round the stands wondering how the toy fair could possibly be ready to open the next day.

They soon decided it was not much like their idea of a fair, but then it was not much like anything, except perhaps a great cavernous lumber room, or some kind of mad factory. There were few toys to be seen yet, and most of the people there seemed to be building elaborate structures of wood and hardboard on their stands, which entailed a lot of hammering and bad language. There seemed to be hundreds of people milling around, banging and shouting and fiddling with lights, all getting hopelessly in each other's way. The children began to think that it was not half the fun they had expected.

In the middle of the hall, however, they found an enormous model railway, and they stayed for some time watching the men in charge as they set out their entire range of engines, rolling stock, stations (with tiny people standing on the platforms) and signal boxes. Both children wished they could control the trains that were being run round to test the circuits, but when they edged longingly towards the elaborate control panel, the men ignored them.

Martin and Lucy turned reluctantly away at last and found that other stands were now beginning to look more organized. They drifted from one to another, looking at everything and occasionally trying things out at the invitation of friendly exhibitors. There were plenty of toys to try: bicycles made up to look like motorbikes, go-karts, spaceships, all kinds of cars and a remarkable range of weaponry.

'What a lot of war things,' Lucy said wrinkling her nose at a stand covered with guns, tanks, missile launchers and dolls dressed in uniforms.

'Super,' said Martin politely as one of the men on the stand offered him an unpleasantly realistic machine gun, which produced sparks and a rattling noise when he wound a handle on the side. Lucy winced.

'Just like the real thing on the telly, eh?' said the man. 'How about this then?' He wound up a large tank and set it off across the floor of the stand. It climbed over books and up a steep ramp he made with a box and a piece of board, all the while throwing out sparks and puffs of chalk from its guns. Every now and then the turret opened and a little man popped his head up and looked around. Martin suddenly became interested.

'That's good,' he exclaimed. 'You could get one of those guns that shoot out bits of potato and try hitting his head when it comes up!'

The man picked up the tank as if he thought Martin might put his plan into action at once.

'Don't you think that would be rather destructive?' he said stiffly.

'Don't see what else you could do with it except just *look*,' Martin muttered to Lucy as they moved on.

'Look, that might be good,' said Lucy.

She pointed to a stand which had been built up to resemble a cave or grotto under a sort of irregular pyramid. It did look interesting. It was covered with glittery stuff in blues and greens and purples. A green dragon with glowing red eyes sat on top, and there seemed to be lighted portholes here and there in the closed sides. Over the open side of the stand, the cave entrance, was a sign made up of twinkling lights which said THE MAGIC MOUNTAIN.

'Not a very big mountain,' Martin remarked.

They walked round the Magic Mountain peering into the portholes. Each one was covered with glass and through it they saw a small lighted compartment containing some sort of peculiar mechanical toy: a jack-in-the-box with a mad golliwog face, a clown that did slow somersaults round his narrow space, a little dancing skeleton.

'How horrid!' said Lucy.

'It's only plastic,' said Martin looking at her with surprise. 'I wonder how it works. I can't see anything. . .'

'I don't care,' said Lucy. 'They all look like little people shut up in boxes – and ever so unhappy.'

'Don't be daft,' Martin said amiably.

As she followed her brother round to the front of the stand to look into the cave, Lucy happened to glance up, and was nearly startled out of her wits to see that the dragon's red eyes were swivelling to follow them round.

'Martin!' she squeaked, clutching his arm and pointing up. As Martin looked at the dragon a puff of green smoke came from its grinning jaws.

'Whatever's the matter with you?' Martin demanded shaking himself free. 'It's only someone working it from the inside. Just someone messing about.'

'Sorry,' Lucy muttered, but she now felt very uneasy. There was something unpleasant about the Magic Mountain.

Inside, however, it was neither sinister nor very mysterious. It was full of jokes and party tricks, which did not seem particularly magical to the children, though Martin was interested in how they worked. The man in charge of the stand was definitely the most unmagical character one could imagine. He sat stolidly in the middle of the cave, a stocky, stodgy sort of person with a little moustache. He wore a dark suit and a bowler hat, and he did not look like someone who would 'mess about' with mechanical dragons, Lucy thought.

Nevertheless, when he demonstrated some of his tricks, the man did them very cleverly, and even when he had shown the children how a few of them were done, they could never actually see him do the tricky bits. He did not offer to show them how he managed to produce a bunch of flowers from his bowler hat, however, nor how he could shake live pigeons from his perfectly ordinary and tidy-looking umbrella. The trouble was that he spoilt the effect entirely by being quite expressionless and flat-voiced all the time. It made the whole thing seem rather dull, and the magic words, which ought to have sounded mysterious and exciting, just sounded silly.

They thanked him politely when he had finished, but Lucy remarked that it was a pity all the tricks were faked and not real magic at all.

'You are a twit,' said Martin. 'There's no such thing as real magic.'

The man smiled faintly at that, but Lucy turned away.

'How can you say that?' she hissed when Martin followed her. 'What about Snowy and all that? That's real isn't it?'

'It might not be,' Martin retorted argumentatively. 'Perhaps we dreamt it.'

'Two people can't have the same dream!' Lucy gasped, nearly speechless with indignation. 'You know it really happened!'

'Dad says that seeing can't always be believing,' Martin said obstinately. 'And anyway, you wouldn't expect me to talk about it in front of that bloke, would you? He'd think we were potty!'

They continued their tour of the toy fair in a prickly silence.

It may have been due to her annoyance with Martin, or perhaps the recollection of Snowy did it, but whatever the cause, the uneasiness Lucy had felt at the Magic Mountain stand stayed with her. Those little jiggling figures shut up in their portholes had made her feel thoroughly miserable, and now she found herself hating everything mechanical that she saw. A lot of the bright, noisy, up-to-date toys they had seen before had turned out to be less interesting than they had appeared, but now Lucy felt almost physically revolted as she approached stands displaying anything of that sort. Cold, she thought, cold and depressing. When she felt herself entering a very cold area, she knew that they must be coming to some notably unpleasant machinery. She was surprised, therefore, to see a stand crowded with dolls. She stopped and stared at them for a moment – and then she saw what was wrong.

'Look,' she said nudging Martin, who was not at all interested in dolls. 'They're all mechanical!'

There was something at the back of her mind about mechanical dolls. Something very disagreeable: something Snowy had said.

A tall severe lady on the stand smiled thinly at her.

'They're quite something, aren't they?' she said.

They certainly were. There were dolls that walked and talked, but there were also dolls that rode bicycles, dolls that played pianos, baby dolls that lay on their backs and kicked, and big dolls that rocked their own little dolls.

'I think this is the best one,' the lady went on. 'How would you like this for Christmas?'

She stood a very large doll in a beautiful gauzy dress on a table

33

in the middle of the stand. At once it started to dance stiffly to a tinkly tune that came from its own inside. After that it sang a nursery rhyme in a sickly, babyish voice, and made a number of pointless remarks. When the performance was over the lady sat it down.

'What do you think of that?' she asked them.

'Jolly good,' said Martin vaguely. His own opinion was that all the dolls were pretty silly. They had nasty smug faces and looked stupid. Lucy only smiled and nodded, tugging at her brother's sleeve to make him come away.

She had remembered what Snowy had said.

'What's the matter now?' Martin said following her. 'Why did you want me to look at those potty dolls anyway?'

'They're all mechanical,' Lucy repeated. 'They're not like proper dolls at all. You couldn't play with things like that dancing doll.'

'I wouldn't want to,' Martin said loftily. Lucy ignored him.

'It's like you said about the tank – all you could do with it would be wind it up, or whatever you have to do, and watch it do all that stuff. And the talking is silly too. If you have an ordinary doll, you can pretend it says anything you like, but that one just says silly things like "Look at me Mummy".'

'You could pretend with it just the same, couldn't you?' Martin said looking a little more interested. Lucy shook her head emphatically.

'No,' she insisted. 'It's all wrong!'

'Well I thought they were fairly nasty,' Martin said. 'But I thought girls liked that sort of thing.'

'You know I don't,' Lucy said crossly. 'They *are* nasty. And I think they've been got at,' she added darkly.

Martin stared at her.

'Got at?' he repeated blankly. 'Who's got at them?'

'The Green Lady!' Lucy whispered urgently. 'They're all cold and lifeless – like Snowy said the things in Captain Lovell's house were – and they're all mechanical, and *all* the mechanical toys feel the same. And Snowy said – '

'What a lot of old rubbish!' Martin scoffed, pushing his hands into his pockets and turning away. 'You're absolutely cracked about all that, aren't you? And why should she bother with *toys*, even if it was true?'

'It's not rubbish!' Lucy said angrily. 'I can feel it. I don't know why she's doing it, but I bet she spoils anything she can get hold of.'

Martin was unconvinced, and they returned to the Friendly Toys stand arguing furiously.

They found Mrs Marsh and Aunt Bea picnicking in the middle of a crowd of soft toys. There were rag dolls, every one an individual and different from all the rest, teddy bears in all sizes and a vast variety of other animals: felt animals, furry animals, woolly animals – all in bright colours and all very friendly. Very *warm* and friendly, Lucy thought with satisfaction, toys to be played with.

'*There* you are, then,' said Aunt Bea. 'I was just beginning to wonder what had become of you. Don't you want any lunch? We've got sandwiches and coffee here.'

While Aunt Bea organized the food, Lucy examined the Friendly Toys.

'Do you like them?' Mrs Marsh asked anxiously. 'I'm afraid they must seem very old-fashioned compared to all the other things you've seen.'

'I think they're nicer than anything else here,' Lucy said.

'That's very nice to hear,' said Mrs Marsh, 'though actually we've got something a little more ambitious this year.'

She picked up a large teddy bear with thick dark brown fur. Lucy was not quite sure what it was about the creature, but she did not like it nearly as much as the other toys on the stand. There was something about its face that she did not care for. Mrs Marsh did something to the bear and put it into Lucy's arms.

35

In a voice very much like a gruffer version of the dancing doll's, it started to sing *The Teddy Bear's Picnic*.

Lucy jumped as if the thing had bitten her.

Next morning Lucy hurried into the living room before breakfast and leaned against the dresser staring up at the little green jug.

'Snowy!' she whispered urgently. 'Snowy, please come down!' But the china cat showed not the slightest sign of life. Martin came into the room and Lucy swung round to face him. He raised his eyebrows at the dresser and shook his head in a most irritating manner.

'You're stupid,' Lucy said miserably.

She hated quarrelling with Martin, but he did not seem to mind. He shrugged and tapped his forehead significantly. It was fortunate that Aunt Bea came trundling in from the kitchen with the trolley at that moment.

'Now then,' she said briskly, 'are you two scrapping again? I heard you yesterday having a regular old go at each other. What's the matter with you?' Without waiting for a reply she started to lay the table and went on: 'I got the impression that Lucy didn't care much for the modern toys yesterday, so I thought you might like to see some very old ones before you go home. I don't think you've ever been to the Whyttington Museum have you?'

The museum was not far from where Aunt Bea lived, and as they walked to it across the park, she explained (or rather did not quite explain) that it was concerned mainly with the history of London, but that the exhibition of historical toys which they were going to see had been arranged specially for the school holidays.

In the entrance hall of the museum there were racks of postcards and on a table was a pile of catalogues for the toy exhibition. Aunt Bea bought one and they looked through it before going to look at the toys themselves. It was a very glossy production, more like an illustrated history of toys, and Lucy studied the pictures of the dolls with satisfaction.

'They look like proper dolls,' she said. 'They don't look all that smart some of them, but they've all got nice faces. They look as if they've lived with children.'

Aunt Bea agreed with her, but Martin sniffed and strolled on ahead of them with his hands in his pockets. He hardly looked at the dolls, but went on to an array of musical boxes, musical clocks and miniature organs, some of which had been set up so that they played when you put a penny in a slot on the display case. Before Aunt Bea and Lucy had finished with the toys, he had wandered on into the galleries concerned with history.

Martin had noticed nothing peculiar about the dolls in his cursory glance, but to Lucy they were very disappointing. There was something wrong with them. They were the dolls shown in the catalogue all right, but somehow they did not look the same. Aunt Bea noticed it too.

'I'm afraid they're not as nice as their photos,' she said. 'Perhaps they did something with the light to make them look better in the catalogue.'

They stood in front of the dolls trying to decide exactly what it was that was different. It was not their faces, but their expressions, Aunt Bea suggested, but that was absurd of course, it *must* be the lighting – and all the time Lucy grew more worried. It was not simply the fact that the dolls did not look like their pictures that upset her, it was what they *did* look like. Every one of them wore the smug expression of the dancing doll at the toy fair, and the whole room felt distinctly chilly.

Lucy left Aunt Bea talking to an attendant about the toys and hurried after Martin, hoping that if she told him about the dolls' faces he would understand her fears. He was not in the Roman London gallery, and she was about to go on to Medieval London, when he suddenly appeared from a side room. A board standing by the door announced:

NEW PERMANENT EXHIBITION
THE BODDINGTON-SMYTHE BEQUEST
(Sir Archibald Boddington-Smythe, 1851–1939)

Martin looked hastily up and down the Roman room, saw Lucy and almost ran across to her. Glancing over his shoulder at the Boddington-Smythe door he dragged her as far away from it as they could get.

'She's in there!' he whispered.

Lucy stared at him without comprehension. His face was white and he seemed very agitated.

'She's in a case all by herself in the middle of that room,' he went on breathlessly. 'It feels like you said about the stuff at the toy fair, only worse – like cold pins and needles all over – like Snowy said. . .'

He looked back again, as if he half expected someone to follow him out of the other room, then he led Lucy cautiously back to it.

'Look round as if you're not interested in anything in particular,' he warned her, 'and don't look surprised when you see *her*.'

The children returned to the Boddington-Smythe room and started to work their way round the cases against the walls. Sir Archibald had apparently devoted his long life to collecting all manner of Oriental bits and pieces, from small articles of jewellery to fairly large statues. As a note on the first case by the door remarked, it was 'a record of the journeys and interests of a great traveller'. Lucy, however, took in very little of it, for she was conscious all the time of the case behind her, at which she had not yet so much as glanced. When he felt that they had paid convincing attention to the rest of the collection, Martin turned to the middle of the room.

They walked slowly round the display case, studying the solitary figure that occupied it: a statue of a woman, about eighteen inches high, made of pale frosty green stone.

There was very little detail in the statue. The Lady was straight and narrow. She seemed to be dressed in a simple robe, which

fell in long formal folds from her shoulders to the ground, con-
cealing her hands and feet. Her features were barely sketched on
the smooth oval of her face – high arched eyebrows over closed
eyes, tiny nose and mouth hardly more than suggested. As the
children examined the statue, their initial surprise and fear began

to wear off a little, though the cold uncomfortable atmosphere was still strong in the room. They could not decide whether the Lady's hair was done up in bobbly curls all over her head, or whether she was wearing some kind of headdress, and they had just started to discuss this, as if she were any ordinary piece of statuary in a museum, when Martin glanced at her face and froze again. The Lady's eyes seemed to be closed, but he was sure he had seen a cold glitter under the drooping lids.

Back at Aunt Bea's flat the children laid the table for lunch.

'Well?' Lucy demanded, clattering the knives and forks triumphantly.

'All right,' said Martin. 'You may have been right about the toys, but I still don't get it.'

'Perhaps that wasn't the Green Lady, then. Perhaps we only imagined. . .' Lucy continued sarcastically.

'I said you were right!' Martin snapped, slamming down the table mats. 'Now shut up about it!'

'We've got to decide what to do next,' Lucy said calmly and straightened the mats with irritating preciseness. 'We've found out where she is – now what?'

Martin wandered over to the dresser and took down the green jug.

'He said we've got to take him home with us,' he said stroking the cat with one finger, 'so that's the next thing we've got to do.'

'But what shall we say to Aunt Bea?' Lucy said.

'Mum says you mustn't ask for things in other people's houses, so we can't say anything anyway,' said Martin righteously. Lucy stared at him.

'You don't mean . . . ? But that's even worse – just *taking* something. That's stealing!' she objected. Martin looked obstinate.

'It can't be,' he insisted, 'because Snowy's a person, and a person can't belong to someone else, so it doesn't matter what Auntie . . .'

Aunt Bea came into the room, stopped short and surveyed them with pursed lips.

'Not again surely?' she sighed. 'You seem to have done nothing but argue. . .' She caught sight of the jug in Martin's hands and at once broke off. 'There now,' she said, taking it from him, 'I'd nearly forgotten about the Snowy jug. I might have let you go without it.'

The children stared at her.

'Why do you call it that?' Martin asked her. Aunt Bea laughed and frowned at the same time as if she were trying to remember something.

'There was a jug just like this in my grandmother's china cabinet when I was a little girl,' she said, 'and we always used to call *that* the Snowy Jug – I can't remember why. I don't know what happened to it when she died – I don't suppose for a minute that this is the same one, but when I saw it in the junk shop the other day, I just had to buy it – it was so much like Snowy.' She looked at the little cat, biting her lower lip as if the thing she could not quite remember were only just out of reach. 'Well anyway,' she went on, shaking her head, 'I thought Lucy might like it, and I wanted you to show it to your Granddad to see if *he* remembers it too.'

3

WHATEVER HAPPENED
TO CAPTAIN LOVELL?

IN the days before the railway, No. 28 Akeman Street, Dunsley, had been a coaching inn. The old stable was still standing, though it was now used as a workshop and garden shed and the loft above it was slowly filling up with junk. The house really belonged to Grandfather Lovell, but after his wife's death he had decided that the place was too big for him, and so he had handed it over to his son, Dr Lovell, who was a lecturer at a London college, and moved himself into a little flat over the archway that had once admitted coaches to the inn yard.

'It will be good for the children to grow up in the country,' Dr Lovell had said when discussing the move with his wife.

'It'll be good for us, too,' said Mrs Lovell. 'But you'll loathe being a commuter.'

'On balance I think commuting is a little less awful than living in London,' Dr Lovell insisted. 'I shan't complain.'

About once a fortnight he arrived home late and complaining bitterly about the station bus, the trains, the stupidity of people who detained him at college until the rush hour was in full spate, when he might have got away early. On these occasions Mrs Lovell said nothing – very pointedly.

As soon as they arrived home from Aunt Bea's, Martin and Lucy went in search of their grandfather, to see if he remembered anything about Snowy. Although old Mr Lovell no longer had any interest in the house, the stable and the garden were still his domain, and the children found him in his greenhouse, which

stood in the walled orchard beyond the part of the garden that had once been the yard.

Grandfather's reaction to the jug was almost exactly the same as Aunt Bea's. He laughed, scratched his head, said, 'Well, well,' several times and turned it round in his hands, staring at it as though there were something particularly odd about it which he was sure he would remember in a minute.

'Well I never did,' he said at last, shaking his head and giving up his attempt to remember whatever it was. 'Fancy that! Of course your Aunt Bea's quite right, it can't possibly be the same jug. But,' he laughed again, 'I never saw anything more like that old Snowy.'

He handed the jug back to Lucy.

'Granddad,' said Martin, 'can you tell us anything about Captain Lovell?'

'Captain Lovell? Do you mean *my* old Granddad?' said Grandfather. 'Has this jug got you interested in family history then?'

The children nodded. Grandfather pushed his spectacles up onto his forehead and looked thoughtful.

'Well now,' he said, 'I didn't get to know him all that well myself, but of course I heard a lot about him from my father.'

'Did he ever say anything about a Green Lady?' Lucy asked cautiously.

'Aha! So you've already unearthed some of the old tales, have you? That's your Aunt Bea, I'll bet,' said Grandfather grinning at her. He sat down on a stool.

'Let's see,' he went on in the sort of voice that promised a story. 'My father didn't have any time for all that Green Lady stuff, but we heard some marvellous tales from my two aunts, his sisters. They used to say this statue that Granddad brought home from India had a curse on it and all that sort of thing. They reckoned that everything changed the minute it came into the house – it created an evil atmosphere. Then they were burgled while Granddad was away, and when he came home my Grandmother insisted he should sell it, because *she* believed it was unlucky too. But getting rid of it didn't do the family's luck any good, because Granddad's ship was wrecked in the Pacific on his next voyage and he disappeared. Maybe that Green Lady took offence at being sold.'

Lucy and Martin looked at each other in surprise.

'We didn't know about the wreck,' Martin said. 'When did it happen?'

'Oh, eighty years ago or more, I'd say. It was when my father was a little boy, anyway,' said Grandfather. '*I* never saw this Lady of yours.'

'But you said,' Martin frowned intently, 'you said you didn't know Captain Lovell *well*, which must mean that you did know him. But if he disappeared when your father was only a little boy . . .'

' . . . *that* must mean he turned up again,' Grandfather finished the sentence for him. 'So he did – thirty years after he disappeared. He couldn't explain where he'd been, or how he got home, and he didn't stay long. It was shortly after my Grandmother died, I remember, and finding her gone and everything different from what it had been like when he left (it was at the end of the first war, or not long after, and everything was all mixed up), he must've decided it wasn't much of a home any more for him. Anyway, nobody knew where he went to, any more than they knew where he'd been for the best part of thirty years – and nobody ever saw him again.'

The children stared at their grandfather.

'Bit of a poser, isn't it?' he said chuckling. 'But that's not all. The most peculiar part of it was that *he* thought he'd only been gone a few months. He didn't look like a man of over seventy either – my father said he didn't look a day older than when he'd last seen him in fact. My father used to talk about loss of memory – but that wasn't it y'know: when Granddad was alone with us children he seemed to remember plenty. Only it didn't make a lot of sense. . .' His voice trailed away and he looked puzzled again, as if he had thought of something important and forgotten it again all in a moment.

'What did he say?' Lucy breathed.

'I'm just trying to remember,' said Grandfather staring at the jug in her hands. 'He never said much about the actual wreck. One minute he was in the middle of the most violent storm he'd ever known, the next he was lying on a sandy beach and the sun was shining. He thought he must have been washed up on a South Sea island, but when he went inland a bit to explore, he said it looked more like the South Downs than the South Seas. There was open downland rising up from the coast, and further inland the hills were heavily wooded.

'Then when he started to explore more widely, he found that it wasn't an island at all. He started walking along the coast, and he reckoned he walked for a couple of weeks without seeing any signs of an end to it, so he concluded that it must be a sizeable chunk of land. Only there shouldn't have been anything like it within hundreds of miles of where he thought he was.

'All the time he'd been walking he hadn't seen a soul, so now he struck inland, hoping he might find someone who could tell him where he was. But there was no one – not a sign of human life anywhere. In the end he decided there wasn't any point in wandering around for ever, and so he found a nice spot by a lake, where he built himself a shack and settled down for a rest. He had an idea too that he might be able to work out his position roughly from the stars.'

Grandfather frowned.

'This was just about the queerest bit of all,' he said slowly. 'If I understood him right – and mind you, it was all of fifty years ago and I was only a lad – the stars were all wrong. There were constellations he recognized, but they were all slightly different from the way he knew them, and there were other stars he didn't know at all. His observations weren't all that accurate of course, he had to improvise instruments and estimate his measurements – all the same, he knew what the sky should have looked like in those parts, and it didn't.

'He used to spend hours trying to work it out when he got home, and just before he disappeared again he said to me one day, "Joe, I think I've got it – it's *askew* to this world!" Now what do you suppose he meant?'

The children shook their heads.

'Did he ever say how he got home?' Lucy asked.

'That was another funny thing,' said Grandfather. 'All he'd ever say about that was that Someone came along after a while and showed him the way. But no one could find out how he'd come. He just turned up on the doorstep one morning. Thought his family must have moved at first, because he didn't recognize anyone – poor old chap.'

'I wonder where on earth he got to,' Lucy said.

Grandfather looked at her oddly.

'It's funny you should put it like that,' he said, 'because *we* used to think it wasn't anywhere on earth at all! And you know, I still believe that when he went off again he was trying to get back there – wherever it was. Anyway,' he chuckled and shook his head, 'if you're thinking of looking for that Green Lady, you'd better be careful – and don't tell your Aunt Bea. She used to believe everything, curse and all, and I bet she still does. You stick to the old Snowy jug – that won't bring you any trouble.'

When they left Grandfather, Lucy and Martin took the jug indoors and put it in Lucy's room. They then made their way to the loft above the stable.

The loft was used indiscriminately for storing things that might be wanted later and dumping things that no one was ever going to want again. It smelt of old furniture and books, of apples arranged on narrow shelves along the walls and strings of onions and bunches of herbs hanging from the rafters. It was one of the children's favourite places, and they kept their diaries and anything else that was particularly secret in an ancient roll-top bureau that stood in one corner. Martin now sat himself down at the bureau and recorded their meeting with Snowy in a new notebook. Lucy sat on an old sofa trying to draw a white cat, and reminding him from time to time of things he might have forgotten. When he had finished Snowy's story, Martin started to write down what Grandfather had told them about Captain Lovell as well.

'I wonder what Granddad meant about Captain Lovell not being anywhere on earth,' Lucy said.

'Precisely that,' said a voice from somewhere above their heads. Snowy sat on a beam which ran the length of the roof, grinning mockingly down at them. 'Though I don't suppose he understands it himself these days,' he continued dropping down beside Lucy on the sofa. 'The frailty of the human memory is something that never ceases to astonish me.'

The children simply stared at him, almost as startled as they had been at his first appearance. Snowy craned his neck to look at Lucy's drawing.

'Not bad,' he said condescendingly. 'Would you like me to

sit for you some time? You might make a really good job of it then.'

'Thank you,' Lucy mumbled. The cat grinned at her and then at Martin.

'In fact,' he said, 'by and large, and taking everything into consideration overall – you haven't made a bad start. Not bad at all.'

'We found the Green Lady,' Martin volunteered.

The cat's manner cooled a little.

'That's what I was talking about,' he said testily. 'I may be compelled to be dumb for a large part of the time, but I'm not deaf – or stupid, and I have gathered from what you've said in my hearing that you've found out at least enough to convince you

49

that I'm neither a dream nor a liar.' He glowered at Martin who blushed and fiddled with his pen. 'Now I'd like to hear the whole story.'

'Won't you explain about where Captain Lovell went, first – and how he got back?' Lucy begged.

Snowy fidgeted irritably.

'I don't know that I *can* explain right now,' he said shortly. 'But he got back because Someone found him and sent him back – that's simple enough.'

'That's more or less what Granddad said, but who was the Someone?' Martin asked.

'Someone whose job it is to keep an eye on things in those parts,' said Snowy. 'Now if we might—'

'Then why was it thirty years before he found him?' Martin persisted.

'It wasn't thirty years, it was only six months.' Both children opened their mouths to protest, but before they could speak Snowy hurried on. 'It was six months *There* but thirty years *Here* – the time was askew too you see. No, of course you don't – there's absolutely no point in me trying to explain – you'll just have to wait,' he gabbled.

'Couldn't you tell us what happened to him in the end?' Lucy said meekly.

'Certainly. I helped him to get back There,' Snowy replied calmly.

'You?' Martin exclaimed.

The white cat seemed to swell and stiffen with offended dignity. 'I do happen to be rather more than an animated jug handle, difficult though the idea may be for you to grasp. I arranged for your great-great-grandfather to return, and there he is to this day, passing his time with fishing and mathematical problems, I understand.'

'What?' cried Lucy.

'Don't say "what",' said the cat primly. 'Say "I beg your

pardon" or "really, how remarkable", if you wish to express astonishment – though I can't see why you should.'

'But he must be hundreds of years old,' Martin protested.

'You're very lavish with your hundreds, aren't you?' Snowy said. 'That would be a wild exaggeration even if he had stayed in this world all his life.' He stretched and yawned. 'But after all his comings and goings between Here and There, it would be quite a business to work out exactly how old he *is*. Since it doesn't seem to worry him I don't see why it should worry you.'

He stood up and stretched again.

'You're not going already are you?' Martin asked anxiously. 'There's hun— masses of things we wanted to ask you. . .'

'*I* have been trying unsuccessfully to get some answers out of *you*,' Snowy said. 'So now, to encourage you to tell me at last what I want to know – and to save you having to tell it twice – we are all three going.'

'Where?' Lucy asked eagerly.

'To see Sarah,' said the cat making for the head of the stairs. 'She should have shut up the shop by now and we may get some tea out of her.'

'Sarah?' the children exclaimed together.

Snowy stopped and grinned at them over his shoulder.

'Your next-door neighbour – I thought she was a friend of yours,' he said. 'Don't you want to tell her about all the excitement you've had in the last few days?'

'She wouldn't believe it,' said Martin doubtfully.

'No? Well, we can but try,' Snowy said.

As the white cat had said, Sarah Peach, who was a potter and lived next-door on the other side of the archway, was a particular friend of the Lovell children. Next-door had once been two little cottages, but they had been knocked together for Sarah, and part of the ground floor had been turned into a shop and pottery. In the shop she sold the things she made herself and a whole lot of

other bits and pieces too – pots and pans, glasses, baskets, prints, toys – anything cheerful or useful that took her fancy.

When they arrived at her back door, Sarah was tidying up the pottery. She was a tall girl with long red hair hanging down her back in a single thick plait. In her jeans and the dark blue smock she wore for messy work she looked like another overgrown child. She called to them to come in and met them in the kitchen, still drying her hands.

'How was the Great Metrollops?' she inquired. 'I suppose you've come to scrounge some tea—'

She broke off suddenly and stared at Snowy, who had jumped up on a chair and was surveying her critically. After a moment of silence the cat sighed.

'You know,' he said conversationally, 'I'm beginning to get used to having old friends stare at me in mute amazement and then pretend they don't remember a thing about me. I suppose it's all one deserves for placing any confidence in human friendship, but I hope you're not going to be another of them.'

Sarah threw her towel down on the table and said:

'It's all right, I've never known another creature as rude as you, so I'm not likely to mistake your identity.'

'Jolly good,' said Snowy comfortably. 'Now, were you going to offer us some tea?'

'You're an ungracious beast,' Sarah remarked amiably. The children looked on in amazement and Snowy suddenly rounded on them.

'It's rude to stare,' he said, fixing them with his bright blue gaze. 'Did you think you were the only people I've ever honoured with my conversation?' He turned back to Sarah. 'What about tea then?' he demanded.

'I don't see why I should be expected to provide tea for *such* an ungracious beast,' Sarah said filling the kettle. 'Don't you think you could possibly be nice to us, at least until we've sorted ourselves out a bit?'

Smiling complacently Snowy settled himself on the chair, tucked his paws in and closed his eyes. Martin turned to Sarah.

'How do you know Snowy?' he demanded.

Sarah looked at the cat, who yawned and said:

'Oh, go on, tell them all about it. They won't pay any attention to anything else until you do.'

'O.K.,' said Sarah. 'When I used to come to Dunsley as a kid to stay with my aunt at Home Farm, there wasn't anyone to play with most of the time, and I used to get pretty bored. But my aunt had this little jug – '

'They know about the jug,' Snowy interrupted. 'That's why I'm back – they brought it here.'

'Well then, that's all there is to it really,' Sarah said. 'Snowy used to come now and then when I was on my own, and sometimes he took me places . . .' she frowned as if she had remembered something strange. 'I hadn't seen him since my aunt left Dunsley,' she continued, 'and I'm afraid I'd forgotten everything until he came in with you just now.'

'What places did he take you to?' Martin asked jealously.

'Oh, places . . .' Sarah looked very vague. Snowy grinned irritatingly.

'To the present home of your great-great-grandfather, the Captain, among other places, he said.

'Oh,' said Lucy, 'can we—'

'Now that your curiosity is satisfied,' said Snowy, knowing perfectly well that it had only been increased, 'can we have that tea?'

Sarah poured some tea into a saucer of milk and put it down for Snowy, before pouring out her own and the children's. She took a ginger cake from the cupboard and cut three large slices. Snowy looked up from his saucer and Sarah broke a corner off her cake and offered it to him.

'I've never known a cat like that one,' she said. 'He'll eat absolutely anything, you know!'

(Martin thought that if *he* had to say which of Snowy's personal characteristics distinguished him from the mass of cats, he would not start with his appetite. Sarah seemed to take a lot for granted.)

'Now, is this a purely social call – looking up old friends and all that – or is there more to it?' she went on.

'We've got to help Snowy get rid of the Green Lady,' Martin told her. Sarah raised her eyebrows.

'Have we, indeed?' she said. 'Well, if this cat wants *me* to lend a hand in his private feuds, he'll have to make a stronger appeal to old acquaintance than he has so far. Anyway, according to the tale he told me she disappeared years ago.'

'It's not a private feud,' Snowy said grimly. 'I admit I have some hope of freeing myself in the course of settling with her – I realize that might not carry much weight with you – ' he glared at Sarah, who muttered:

'I'm not sure that it wouldn't be a positively bad idea to give you any more freedom.'

' – But the main objective is to thwart a plan which would have the most unpleasant consequences for the whole of humankind. She has reappeared and is already at work.'

He jumped onto his chair again and started to wash his face.

'It's true,' said Lucy urgently. 'We've seen her, and felt . . .' she shivered, not daring to recall too much of that feeling.

'Tell me more,' said Sarah curiously.

The children told her about the toy fair, Lucy's unease, the strange similarity of the two sets of dolls and the discovery of the Lady.

'Only we don't see why she should have anything to do with the toy fair,' said Martin. 'So perhaps it wasn't—'

'I can see why,' Sarah said. 'It seems pretty obvious. Children have bags of imagination – she gets at their toys, draws off all that energy, and then she's also got *them* tied up for the rest of their lives. Right?'

She looked at Snowy.

'I think you are,' he said. 'She would seem to have hit on a neat idea there – very neat and very nasty. Unfortunately it's not the nastiest thing she's thought up.'

Sarah frowned and seemed to be about to say something, but Martin got in first.

'Snowy says that it's all going to happen here,' he said.

'Really?' said Sarah looking at the children thoughtfully. 'So it's going to end in Dunsley with the Lovells – as it began.' She turned to Snowy. 'What makes you so sure? It makes a nice tidy story of course, but I imagine there must be more to it than that.'

'Oh yes,' said the cat, 'there's a very simple, practical reason why I'm certain that it'll end here, one way or the other. As I've said before, the Lady is evidently thinking of something a little more unpleasant for humankind than a bit of dullness and discomfort. She has a scheme to make herself supremely powerful in this world – a very dangerous scheme, but to carry it out she needs one very special object, and to the best of my knowledge that object is somewhere in this locality (a fortuitous coincidence, if you believe in that sort of thing, which I don't). I intend to get to it first.'

'What is it and what's she going to do?' Martin demanded.

The cat shifted restlessly, looking about as if he thought someone might be spying on them.

'That must wait. I'll show you soon,' he said. 'There are other things we must do first. We have to gather up our forces. We must find the Fiddler.'

'The Fiddler?' said Sarah. 'You mean the bronze statue of the old man? How do we do that? I suppose we could start by combing all the antique shops in the country—'

'That won't be necessary,' Snowy said. 'That was only a temporary disguise. Last time I saw him he was a highly respectable and perfectly normal person – well, not altogether conventional, perhaps, but flesh and blood at least.'

'Why don't we put an advertisement in the newspapers,' Martin suggested eagerly. 'You know, the sort of thing that sounds nonsense except to the person it's meant for.'

'Marvellous,' said Sarah. 'Personal Column of *The Times*, I should think. I've always wanted to do that.' She pulled open a drawer in the kitchen table and started to hunt through it. 'What's the name then?' she asked emerging with a pencil and a piece of paper.

'Schwartz,' said Snowy. 'William Schwartz – a professional violinist. I don't see anything so very surprising about that.'

He cocked his head on one side and looked quizzically at Sarah, for she had started to write the name down, and then stopped and stared at him.

'Is that so?' she said slowly. 'You know, I think we might try the *Irish Times* as well.'

Snowy pricked his ears.

'What do you know?' he demanded.

'I'm not sure,' Sarah replied shaking her head, 'but I remember that my father had a friend called William Schwartz who was a violinist and went to live in Ireland some years ago. It would be an extraordinary coincidence—'

' – But no more extraordinary than anything else in this affair,' Snowy chimed in. 'You're quite right: it's well worth trying. Really, you are all turning out to be quite a credit to me all of a sudden.'

'What a cheek!' Sarah cried, seizing her discarded towel and threatening him with it. 'Can't you even pay a compliment without trying to corner most of it for yourself?'

Snowy leapt to the floor and ran to the back door which stood slightly ajar. Looking back over his shoulder he said:

'By the way, could you try to be free next Sunday afternoon?' And then he slipped round the door.

'Wretched cat!' Sarah exclaimed, jumping to her feet. As she did so she knocked her mug over, and by the time she had picked it up and reached the door there was not a trace of a cat to be seen in the garden. As Sarah returned to mop up her spilt tea, grumbling about Snowy all the time, the children heard the gate under the arch rattle. Mrs Lovell put her head round the door.

'I thought I'd find them here,' she said. 'Are they pestering you, Sarah?'

'They're as good as gold,' Sarah told her winking at the children.

'Remarkable!' said Mrs Lovell. 'They can come and emulate gold at home now – they start school again tomorrow and I don't want them running around until all hours looking for things they kicked into corners three weeks ago and absolutely must find by nine o'clock tomorrow morning.'

4

HENRY AND THE
CONJUROR'S BOX

UNDER normal circumstances Sarah allowed the Lovell children
to spend as much time as they liked in the pottery, as long as they
did not interfere with her work in any way. During the next few
days, however, they were hardly out of the place when they
were not at school, and they badgered Sarah to tell them about
her childhood adventures with Snowy, until she threatened to ban
them from her premises until Sunday if they did not drop the
subject.

'I've told you – I only have the dimmest memory of it all. And
I don't know how much really happened and how much I made
up myself later,' she said.

'But you must be able to remember *something*,' Lucy pleaded.
'Like whether you met anyone else besides Captain Lovell. . .'

'As a matter of fact I did,' Sarah said reluctantly. 'But I don't
suppose you'd believe me if I told you about it.'

The children assured her fervently that they would.

'All right then,' she said. 'There was this large – very large –
black and white striped mouse who lived on a sort of tropical
island and did card tricks. I think he played the ukelele too. His
name was Jerome and he had a brother called Sylvester. There
was a whole colony of these striped mice. . .'

She looked sternly at the children, daring them to disbelieve
her. Martin suddenly spluttered with laughter.

'There,' she said crossly. 'I knew you wouldn't believe
me.'

'It's not that,' said Martin. 'It's just that when Snowy said we should tell you about meeting him, we thought you wouldn't believe us – we didn't know you had met a mouse that did card tricks.'

Sarah smiled slowly.

'Well, as I said, I'm not sure that I really did meet it,' she said. 'And I don't see how the bits I can remember fit what you've told me. The differences in time, for instance – there *was* something odd about that, but I think it must have been the other way round: I was There longer than I was away from Here. It couldn't have been the way it was for Captain Lovell, because nobody ever noticed that I'd been gone at all.'

'Perhaps it wasn't the same Other Place,' Martin suggested.

'Oh, that would make it all too complicated for words!' Sarah exclaimed despairingly. 'It must have been the same. But even then I don't see what any of it has to do with the Green Lady business. Unless the Other Place comes into her mysterious plan involving the mysterious something that we are mysteriously going to find. I can't make head or tail of it myself.

'However, I don't think we're very likely to guess what's going on, so we might as well drop the subject for now, and hope that our feline friend will be more forthcoming when next we meet.'

On Sunday Sarah invited the children to have lunch with her, and asked Mrs Lovell if she might take them out in the afternoon. They were finishing lunch and discussing the advertisement Sarah was going to put in the newspapers, when they heard a scratching at the kitchen window. Snowy was sitting outside on the sill.

'You're too late,' Sarah said, opening the window for him. 'We've finished lunch.'

'There's still some ice-cream left, I see,' the cat remarked as he stepped in with whiskers twitching delicately.

'Isn't that just about the limit?' Sarah demanded, putting her dish on the floor for him. 'Snatching the food out of my mouth now.'

'Are you going to take us to the Other Place?' Lucy asked eagerly. 'How shall we get there?'

'We're not going that far and Sarah's van will be quite adequate transport,' Snowy said, licking a drop of ice-cream from his whiskers. 'As adequate as it ever is,' he added.

'If you don't like it . . . ,' Sarah began threateningly.

'My dear, I think it's admirable,' Snowy said in a soothing tone. 'I mean, the way you keep it going. . . Now what about this advertisement?'

He jumped onto a chair at the table and reached out a paw for the piece of paper on which they had been trying out their ideas. Sarah picked it up.

'We decided to keep it very short and ordinary-sounding – trivial,' she said. She offered the paper to Snowy and he read:

'WILLIAM SCHWARTZ, violinist – have found your white cat – Sarah Peach.' His tail fluffed and twitched a little. 'Well, thank you,' he said. 'I'm glad you think I sound sufficiently trivial.'

Sarah grinned and pretended to score herself a point on the wall.

'You know what I mean,' she said. 'Now how about telling us what we're supposed to be doing this afternoon.'

'I seem to remember you used to be very fond of Folly Wood,' Snowy said casually. 'I thought we might drive up there for a picnic, that's all.'

The children looked disappointed, but Sarah looked searchingly at the cat, and then started to collect up the plates and pile them in the sink.

'I see,' she said, turning on the taps and squirting washing up liquid into the water. 'So we're just going for a nice little picnic? All right, we'll play it your way.'

Sarah's van was an ancient estate car: a tall square vehicle, displaying a considerable area of varnished woodwork. It started noisily and they drove out of Dunsley at a steady pace, climbing the wooded ridge above the town by a narrow lane sunk between high banks. At the top the stretches of woodland were broken up by fields, and after a few minutes they came to an open common. They drove through the straggling village of Chilridge (pronounced 'Chillidge'), and a little further on Sarah pulled off the road onto a track which led into a wood.

'Right,' she said, 'where are we going to have this picnic?'

'I thought we might walk a little way into the wood first,' Snowy said. Sarah shrugged.

'Come on then, kids,' she said. 'We obviously aren't going to get anything out of this animal until he's good and ready.'

They climbed out of the van and followed Snowy into the wood. Presently they came into the open again and found themselves looking at a low hill, on which stood a squat round tower.

'Whatever's that?' Lucy asked. 'Is it going up or coming down?'

'That's the Folly,' Sarah told her. 'It isn't doing either. It was built like that to look like a ruin.'

'How stupid!' Martin said in amazement.

'Precisely,' said Sarah. 'That's why it's called a folly. The wood's named after it.'

'Can we go in?' Lucy asked.

'I shouldn't think so. It always used to be locked up,' Sarah said, but Snowy continued to walk ahead of them up the hill.

'Why don't we go and see?' he suggested, looking back over his shoulder. Sarah eyed him suspiciously but followed.

'There's someone in there,' Martin exclaimed as they approached the Folly. 'I can hear someone whistling.'

The door of the building was open and they could see someone moving about inside. Creeping closer, without knowing quite why they were being so cautious, they saw that there was a kind of workshop inside the Folly occupied by a young man. He was thin with dark curly hair and very bright clothes – yellow and blue checked trousers, a bright blue shirt and a red and white bandana handkerchief tied round his neck.

Suddenly the young man became aware of their presence. He looked up from his work to find himself being solemnly regarded from the doorway by a girl with red hair, two children and a white cat. For a moment they looked almost unearthly, appearing from nowhere and standing there watching him silently, the sun behind them outlining them with brightness.

'Good Lord! An apparition!' he exclaimed.

'You're the one to talk,' Snowy remarked, walking round his feet and eyeing his trousers critically.

'I beg your pardon!' gasped the young man, staring first at the cat and then at the little group by the door.

'Don't mind him,' Lucy said swiftly. 'He's always like that. I think your clothes are lovely.'

'Well, thank you very much indeed,' said the young man crossing slowly to the door. 'Do you kids make a habit of wandering round the countryside commenting on the appearance of complete strangers?'

'It wasn't me,' said Martin indignantly. 'It was him – Snowy.'

'Oh yeah!' The young man's eyes popped and the words emerged as a strangled yelp. 'Steady on now, Henry,' he said unsteadily, untying his bandana and mopping his face with it. 'It's a circus act – the cat's a ventriloquist.'

'Very witty,' said Snowy, and Sarah started to giggle. The young man went very red in the face.

'Look,' he said, 'I may be suffering from the heat, or perhaps you lot are a product of my overstrained brain – ' Snowy sniggered at this and the young man glared at each of them in turn; ' – but whatever you are, would the joker among you please shut his or her trap, and would you all GO AWAY!'

'Your manners seem to be about on a level with your intelligence,' Snowy remarked.

'Cat! *Your* manners are nothing to write home about,' said Sarah. 'For goodness' sake shut up.'

The young man goggled and Snowy stared roundly at her for a second, and then sat himself down by the door and shut his eyes.

'I'm terribly sorry about that,' Sarah said, smiling as warmly as she knew how to and holding out her hand. 'I'm Sarah Peach and these are Lucy and Martin Lovell. I know you won't believe it, but—'

The young man waved her apology aside.

'Youthful high spirits,' he said, trying to smile at Sarah and scowl at the children at the same time.

'It wasn't—' Martin began, but Sarah frowned at him.

'I've never seen anyone here before,' she went on, 'and when we heard you whistling we came across to see if we could get into the Folly. I'm terribly sorry we disturbed you – we'll go at once of course.'

'Good heavens no!' said the young man, seizing Sarah's hand and shaking it enthusiastically. 'It's quite all right. My name's Henry Partridge. Come in and have a look round if you like – there's nothing much to see.'

Henry was being unnecessarily modest. It was true that the large circular room was sparsely furnished, containing only a work bench, two old wardrobes and a couple of wooden boxes, but it was cluttered with tools and bits of machinery, and in the middle of the bench stood something that was certainly worth looking at – a beautiful model of a steam locomotive. It was not really an accurate model of anything that had ever been seen on the railways: it was more like a fantasy on a Victorian steam engine, highly ornamented and shining with brass and enamel. Sarah and the children leaned on the bench and admired Henry's work at great and gratifying lengths.

'You must be the first people who haven't told me I'm wasting my time,' he said bitterly. 'My father calls it "knick-knackeries".'

'Have you got any more?' Martin asked.

Henry opened one of the wardrobes. On the shelves which had been put in from top to bottom stood several more of these fantastical creations, including a little train with two carriages.

'Do you do this for a living?' Lucy asked him. He laughed shortly, but not as if he found the question really amusing.

'No,' he said. 'As my father never ceases to remind me, "There's no living in it".'

'I'm not sure that I agree with him,' Sarah said. 'They're lovely. I know you couldn't make much out of those few, but it would be a start. . .' She ran the tip of her finger along the tank of the engine on the bench and seemed to be thinking hard.

'Who'd buy them?' Henry said, shrugging his shoulders.

'I'm a potter,' Sarah told him, 'but I sell all sorts of stuff as well as my own "knick-knackeries" as your father would say. If you let me take something of yours, I'll put it in my window and we'll see what happens. How about it?'

Henry stared at her. He took the little train out of the cupboard and set it on the bench.

'I suppose it's worth a try,' he said slowly. 'Let's see how this goes.'

'Goes?' shouted Martin.

'Yes, goes,' Henry repeated making a face at him. 'I may be short of wit, manners and intelligence according to you, but my steam engines *go*. They're fired with meths but they're real steam engines.'

Martin bent close to see what Henry did, thinking that he would like to tell Snowy just what he thought of him, since he was certain that the cat had ruined any chance he might have had of making friends with Henry – and to be friends with Henry was what Martin most wanted. The little train crept along the bench puffing prodigiously.

'How lovely!' Lucy exclaimed. 'I bet you could make lots of money out of things like that. More than anything you do now!'

'What *are* you doing now?' Sarah asked.

'Working for my father on the farm. I'm supposed to be making up my mind what I'm going to do,' Henry said glumly. 'The trouble is, the only thing I *want* to do is make these – I've messed up everything else I've tried. I was supposed to be an engineer—'

'Did you ever really try?' Snowy asked from the door.

Henry started and then looked at Martin.

'You're at it again,' he said warningly.

'I'm not,' said Martin and at the same time Snowy said:

'It was I.'

Henry was amazed.

'Now that really is clever,' he said. 'How did you do it?'

Snowy squealed with amusement.

'Isn't he absolutely priceless?' he demanded. 'A talking cat doesn't fit any of his prejudices, but he's prepared to believe Martin's a multi-track ventriloquist. That's Henry all over –

never accept a simple answer you can't understand, if you can find an absurd one you think you do.'

'You're only making things worse,' said Sarah. 'Can't you keep quiet?'

'I was merely making a point, which I felt you should take note of,' said Snowy standing up and stretching. 'Now I shall go back to the van and wait for you there, since you find my company disturbing.'

He walked out with his tail in the air. Henry stared after him and then at Martin.

'It'll be all right now,' said Lucy.

Henry turned to her as if he could not trust himself to know who had spoken.

'Well,' said Sarah trying to smooth things over again, 'let's hope your father will be able to spare you when we've got so many orders that you have to work on your engines full time.'

Henry smiled faintly.

'Father wants to see me in something respectable and secure. He's afraid I'm going to take after my grandfather,' he said.

'What did he do?' Martin asked.

'He was a conjuror on the music halls,' Henry said. 'Made pots of money, I believe, but he wasn't considered at all respectable. The family thinks I must have got my liking for gadgets from him – he was quite famous for some of the ones he used in his act. He had a very clever box. . .'

He went to the second of his cupboards and took from the top shelf something that looked like a wooden model of a classical temple, with a wide carved gable on top and fluted columns on either side of the double doors at the front. It was clearly very old. Henry placed it on the bench and opened the doors.

'It doesn't look all that impressive,' he said, 'but it's very ingenious.'

He put a screwdriver inside, closed the doors and did something at the back of the box. There was a slight clicking from inside and when it stopped he opened the doors again – the box was empty. Henry held up the screwdriver and grinned.

'The mechanism's a bit stiff these days and I'm not very good at working it,' he said apologetically. 'You shouldn't see that I do anything at all to it except shut the doors.' He tapped the inside of the box with the screwdriver. 'The inside rotates and drops whatever is in it out at the back. There's other things you can do with it too – things can be hidden in secret compartments. I'm not sure that I know all its tricks myself.'

Martin's fingers itched to find out all that could be done with the magic box.

'What did your grandfather do with it?' he asked Henry.

'Made things disappear and reappear,' Henry told him. 'Not just oddments from people in the audience either – he had a whole troupe of mice he bred for his act, and they used to go into the box and disappear. It must have been quite dramatic, because they were apparently as big as guinea pigs and striped like zebras!'

'What?' Sarah cried. 'Black and white striped mice?'

Martin and Lucy thought her amazement excessive, even for such an unusual thing as striped mice, but then they too remembered her expeditions with Snowy. They exchanged suspicious glances and looked round for the cat.

'Oh yes,' said Henry evidently pleased with the effect his story had. 'I never saw them myself of course, because he retired before I was born, but I saw photos of them. When I was a kid I used to wish he'd kept them, but the only thing he did keep was this box. My grandmother hated the stage and didn't want anything round the place to remind her of it, as far as I can make out. I think it was a shame. The old man was quite famous in his day – the Great Alectoris and his Oriental Mysteries!'

Henry blew an imaginary fanfare, swirled an imaginary cloak and bowed to his audience of three.

'Some of the stuff he collected as props must have been pretty valuable,' he went on. 'I remember Gran always used to go on about a statue that she swore he bought for her and then took to use in his act – only something funny happened and he said the thing was unlucky (you know how superstitious theatre people are) and sold it. Gran carried on something alarming until the day she died about him selling her Green Goddess behind her back.'

This time it was the children who reacted at once.

'What sort of Green Goddess?' Lucy demanded breathlessly.

'I don't know. What sorts are there?' Henry said laughing. 'It was just what Grandpa called her. I don't suppose she was anything special – just a green stone statue of a woman, by all accounts.'

Suddenly he seemed to remember something and glanced hastily at his watch.

'Good Lord!' he said. 'Is that the time? Look, I'm sorry,' he smiled warmly at Sarah, 'but I'll have to get back home. I seem to be about two hours late for lunch.'

He put the conjuror's box back in the cupboard and he and Sarah started to pack the model train. While they did this, Martin and Lucy wandered round the Folly examining the fascinating bits and pieces of machinery and models which were strewn everywhere. A large something under a tarpaulin particularly interested them. Martin lifted a corner and found basketwork.

'What's this, Henry?' he called.

'A balloon,' said Henry. He crossed the room and pulled aside the tarpaulin, so that they could see the big basket.

'Oh!' said Lucy, clapping her hands to her mouth, 'oh Henry – how lovely! Could we . . . could you . . . ?'

Henry laughed.

'I wouldn't dream of taking you lot up, unless I had the written permission of your parents or legal guardians in triplicate,' he said, 'but in the unlikely event of you securing that, I just might . . .'

Lucy hurled herself on him and hugged him.

'I do think you're nice!' she said.

Martin said: 'Thank you very much,' and added: 'I'm sorry about Snowy,' which was going beyond the call of duty, in his opinion, but he felt that even so remote an offer of a ride in a balloon required something extra in the way of thanks, and he was not in the habit of hugging people.

Henry saw them out of the Folly with the train, and they returned through the woods to the road.

On arrival they discovered that Snowy had found a way into the van, and having also managed to open a packet of sardine sandwiches, had nearly finished his tea already. He looked up, licking his whiskers, as Sarah opened the door.

'You don't happen to have any cheese, do you?' he said.

'Of all the priceless cheek . . .' Sarah exclaimed, grabbing the basket indignantly and lifting it out of the back of the van. The children scrambled in after her and Snowy sat back calmly washing his face while they started on what was left of their picnic.

'Well,' he said, 'has he got it?'

'Got what?' Martin demanded with his mouth full.

'The box of course – the conjuror's box!' Snowy said wearily, as if he'd told them all about it a hundred times. Lucy looked up from the basket with sudden understanding.

'Is *that* the thing you said the Green Lady wants?' she asked.

'And was it her that Henry's grandfather sold?' Martin added.

'And where do the mice come into it?' Sarah said. 'They do come into it, don't they?'

Snowy closed his eyes.

'Yes, yes, and yes in a way,' he said. 'It is there, is it? A sort of temple thing?'

'Yes, it's there,' said Sarah, 'what about it?'

'Thank you,' said Snowy opening his eyes and looking at them. 'You're still doing quite well, you know.'

'That's more than could be said for you,' Sarah said grimly. 'If you wanted to know about the box, why didn't you find out about it yourself? And if you're roping Henry Partridge into your plans, why antagonize him like that?'

'As to the first,' said Snowy, 'I've tried to get in touch with Henry as I have with the rest of you, but it didn't work – he just did not see or hear me. And you saw what happened today – because *you* obviously saw and heard me, he couldn't avoid doing so, but he still wouldn't believe it. I can only contact him through you.

'As for antagonizing him, I think I spoke to him in the way I speak to most people didn't I? Anyway, I wanted you to see what Henry is like – he's got an outstanding talent for credulous disbelief. Like most people who claim to believe only what they can prove, he really means he'll only believe what suits him. So don't ever think you can explain anything to him – it won't work.'

'All right,' said Sarah, 'but when are you going to do some explaining to us? What *is* this box and why does the Lady want it for a start? And what's this plan of hers?'

Snowy sniffed irritably. Martin noticed that questions about the Lady's plan always seemed to upset him.

'It's better not to talk about that too much,' the cat said. 'The box has certain curious properties that even the Great Alectoris didn't know about.' He hesitated and then went on: 'it's a way through to the Other Side – unauthorized – dangerous – shouldn't exist anyway. We'll talk about it when the Fiddler comes.'

And he refused to say another word on the subject.

5

IN WHICH THINGS MOSTLY
FAIL TO HAPPEN

THE children saw no more of Snowy that week, but when they dropped in to see Sarah on their way home from school on Friday afternoon, she had something to show them.

'How about this then?' she said, pushing a letter across the counter to them. It was written in beautiful italic script on fine paper, and was headed with an address in Dublin. The children read:

'My dear Sarah,

I was very sorry to hear of the death of your father last year. I was abroad at the time, and only heard the sad news on my return a few weeks ago. He was a fine artist, and his passing is a great loss to many people besides those of us who were his personal friends.

I have been thinking that it is a long time since I last saw you, and I have been very remiss in discharging my duties as a godfather. It is also many years since I walked in the Chilterns, and I thought I might combine two pleasures by paying you a visit. I will be arriving in the district on May 1st and I am going to presume on old acquaintance by asking you to pick me up at the cross on Chilridge Common at dawn on that day. I know this sounds extremely eccentric, but I have personal – let us say *sentimental* reasons for wishing this.

Your affectionate godfather,

William Schwartz.'

While the children were reading the letter, Sarah wandered to the back of the shop, where an enormous rocking horse stood against the partition between the shop and the pottery. Her father, who had been a sculptor, had made Horse for her when she was a little girl and had modelled him on the horses in an

Oriental picture she had liked – proudly galloping horses in ornate harness and dark greeny blue in colour. Sarah stroked the arched neck absentmindedly, as if he were a live animal.

'Well it must be *your* William Schwartz all right, but is it Snowy's?' Martin asked her when they had finished.

'I think it must be,' said Sarah returning to the counter.

'He doesn't mention Snowy,' Lucy objected.

'That's one reason why I think it's him,' Sarah replied. 'I mean, if he didn't understand the advertisement, he'd say, "what's all this stuff about a cat?", wouldn't he? And there's this.' She showed them an envelope addressed to her in the same hand-writing as the letter. The children stared at it puzzled – there seemed to be nothing wrong with it.

'He sent it here,' Sarah pointed out, 'but there wasn't any address in the advertisement, only a box number, so how did he know it? He wouldn't have had time to find out from anyone, and anyway, I don't know who he'd ask – Mother moved after Father died, so I shouldn't think he'd know her address either.'

They all considered this for some moments. The writer of the letter certainly seemed to be the sort of person who might keep company with the white cat.

'He hasn't wasted much time,' Martin remarked. 'When's May the first?'

'Monday,' said Sarah. 'That's the only thing about it that's at all odd, and even that's covered up a bit. He obviously doesn't want to be seen arriving, but he's tried to make the whole thing seem like an ordinary letter to a goddaughter he hasn't seen for some time.'

Martin's eyes widened.

'In case it got into the wrong hands?' he suggested.

Sarah nodded.

'It does look like that,' she said.

On Saturday afternoon Henry dropped in to ask Sarah if she

would like to go to the cinema that evening. While he was in the shop a man came in and not only bought the little train, but ordered another when he discovered that Henry was the maker. Amazed and delighted, Henry whisked Sarah away to celebrate his first sale. Since he carried her off on Sunday too, for the whole day, Martin and Lucy did not see Sarah again that weekend. They did not see anything of Snowy either.

On Monday morning Sarah drove up to Chilridge about an hour before dawn, and parked by the stone cross just outside the village to wait for the Fiddler. She must have dozed while she waited, for she suddenly realized that it was growing light, and Mr Schwartz had not yet turned up. When it was full daylight she drove through the village and back, but there was no sign of anyone who might have been the missing Fiddler. At about six o'clock a man rode past on a bicycle and a car started in the distance.

Sarah decided that her guest would hardly show up now that people were on the move and so she drove slowly home, keeping an eye on the woods along the road, in case he had decided to wait for her somewhere else, but the only signs of life she saw were a milk delivery van and a red and yellow horse-drawn caravan, which was parked in the woods some distance from the road. She wondered for a moment whether it might be a good idea to stop and ask if anyone had seen an elderly man taking an early morning stroll (she thought she could remember Mr Schwartz well enough to describe him). But then she reminded herself that he must have thought there was some need for secrecy, or he would not have made this odd arrangement. Perhaps he had made his own way to the shop after all, she thought, and would be waiting for her there when she returned. But he was not.

He had not arrived when the children came home from school that afternoon, and he was still missing at the week-end.

On Sunday morning Martin and Lucy sat in Sarah's kitchen,

anxiously wondering what had happened, while Sarah tried to reassure them.

'He must have been unexpectedly delayed,' she said.

'Then why hasn't he written to tell you?' Martin demanded.

'And why hasn't Snowy been around at all? It's a fortnight since we last saw him off the jug,' said Lucy. 'Something must have gone wrong.'

'Oh you know what he's like,' Sarah said. 'It's quite likely that he wouldn't bother to tell us about any change in his plans if we weren't actively involved.'

'Well I think there's something funny going on,' said Martin darkly.

'At least we know where the Green Lady is,' said Lucy.

'True,' said Sarah, 'but there's nothing we can do at the moment. . .'

She spread the Sunday papers out on the kitchen table and offered the children a colour supplement. They turned the pages listlessly while Sarah tried to interest herself in the news. Suddenly she groaned.

'Oh no! Look at this lot!' she said. 'We are no longer the only people to be interested in the whereabouts of the Green Lady. It seems the Curator of the Whyttington Museum and the Metropolitan Police now share our concern!'

She pushed the paper across to the children.

'MYSTERY GODDESS STOLEN,' Lucy read. 'Police baffled . . . mysterious green statue . . . stolen last night from the Whyttington Museum . . . glass case shattered . . . burglar alarms untouched . . . Curator Mr William Boyce says . . . um . . . um . . . recently put on display for the first time . . . didn't know much about her, but the thieves apparently did, since nothing else was taken from this valuable collection.'

There was a small picture of the Lady beside the report.

'Well that's that,' said Martin glumly. 'Now we don't know where *she* is either.'

'Don't we?' said Sarah grimly.

'Do you think she *wasn't* stolen?' Lucy asked.

'What do you think?' said Sarah. 'Case smashed but no alarms set off? No signs of forced entry? It's a funny sort of burglary. But if she's been standing there accumulating energy somehow since she was put on display, she could have burst the case open and simply walked out. Anyway, she's on the loose. And even if we don't know where she is now, we know where she's going to make for, don't we?'

'The box!' Lucy exclaimed. 'She'll be looking for it!'

'No doubt,' said Sarah. 'Unfortunately that wretched cat was so keen on being mysterious that he failed to tell us either what *she* would do with the thing, or what *he* intended to do with it – all would be made plain when the Fiddler arrived – only he hasn't. *We* now have to decide what to do without having the slightest idea of what's going on.'

'We can't tell Henry to hide the box, because he wouldn't believe us,' said Lucy.

'Couldn't we take it and hide it ourselves?' Martin suggested.

Lucy looked doubtful.

'Would that be right?' she said.

'Well it's not stealing – just hiding it for a while,' Martin urged.

Sarah made a face and said:

'I don't know. It seems the simplest way, but if it were as simple as that, wouldn't Snowy have told us to do it right away? And then there's the old question of whether the ends justify the means.'

'What does that mean?' Martin asked sulkily.

'It means that if you try to make something right by doing something wrong, you might spoil the something right, because right and wrong don't mix. And we are supposed to be on the right side – and carrying off other people's property without their permission is usually considered to be wrong,' Sarah explained.

'Even if you only want to keep it safe?' Martin persisted.

'Even then,' said Sarah firmly.

'But even if we don't know exactly what the Lady is going to do with the box, we know that it'll be bad,' Lucy said slowly. 'I think Snowy said she can use it somehow to prevent him and the Fiddler from fighting her, so we ought to do something, or it might be too late when they *do* come. . .'

'Look,' said Sarah, obviously trying to be patient, 'I don't fancy the idea of a vengeful goddess out of the deep past rampaging about with unlimited powers any more than you do – I think it's a rotten idea. But we can't blunder around without knowing what we're up to. I've got a nasty feeling that we could only make things worse by breaking the rules of ordinary civilized behaviour.'

Martin sighed.

'At least we can keep an eye on the box,' he grumbled. 'Henry said he'd help Lucy and me to make a model ship last week. If we take him up on that it would be a good excuse for us to go up to the Folly whenever he's there, and we'd know if anything happened to it.'

Henry had no objections to the idea of the children making a model at the Folly; indeed, he seemed to be flattered by the attention they paid to his instruction and the regularity with which they came for it. Things continued much as before to the end of another week, and another, and if there was still no word from the Fiddler, and Snowy was still immobile, at least they saw nothing of the Green Lady either.

Then on a Friday morning Dunsley woke to sensational news. It arrived at 28 Akeman Street with Mrs Higgs, who came in two mornings a week to clean. She was a tall, angular woman, fiercely energetic, remorselessly talkative and related to three quarters of the town by blood or marriage, which meant that she knew all about everything the minute it happened. This morning she was clearly bursting with happenings.

'Did *you* have any bother then?' she said eagerly as she entered the kitchen.

'Bother, Mrs Higgs?' said Mrs Lovell. 'What sort of bother and when?'

'Last night,' said Mrs Higgs, 'there's been burglaries all over the town!'

'Good Lord!' said Dr Lovell, putting down his paper. '*We* haven't been burgled, have we?'

'No dear,' said Mrs Lovell.

'That's all right, then,' said her husband, and retreated to his study with the paper and a cup of coffee.

'Who's been burgled?' Martin asked.

'Mrs Beddoes at The Yews in Park Road. . .'

'The Yews?' said Mrs Lovell. 'Surely that's where Father-in-law lived years ago. . .'

'Yes,' said Mrs Higgs, 'and Home Farm too. Our Ernie delivers Mrs Beddoes's milk, and her Elsie told him all about it this morning – you know, Elsie Freeman that used to be Jones, she's living in until . . .'

'Yes, I know,' said Mrs Lovell, 'until Mrs Beddoes's niece . . .'

' . . . *cousin* comes, yes,' said Mrs Higgs. 'She was ever so upset – Mrs B. I mean – well Elsie was too, of course. You never saw anything like it, Elsie said. Took the place apart they did. Stuff thrown all over the place. She said they was *looking* for something though, because nothing was taken – everything just thrown about.'

'What about Home Farm?' Martin asked. 'What happened there?'

'Well, same thing more or less, according to our Ernie,' said Mrs Higgs. 'Don't make sense, does it? Breaking things up and chucking them around like that. That's them vandals, I expect.'

'People do some stupid things,' Mrs Lovell agreed, 'some of these boys . . .'

'It might have been the gypsies, of course,' Mrs Higgs went on.

'There's been scores of them around this week, haven't you noticed? If I've answered the door to one I've answered it to a dozen, I'm sure – well, you know, more than one.'

She laughed loudly and tied on her apron.

'I haven't seen any myself,' said Mrs Lovell, 'perhaps they came when I was out.'

'Yes, well, they weren't the usual lot,' said Mrs Higgs, 'and they're not camping in the usual place up the woods. There's nothing up there at the moment, so Arthur says. "Can't imagine where they come from," he says. "They must be sprouting out of the ground." – Laugh! – Well some of them look like it don't they?' Mrs Higgs turned the taps on and started to collect the breakfast things. Mrs Lovell picked up a tea towel.

'We did see a caravan on the common when we went up to see the full moon the other evening,' Mrs Higgs went on, with a suggestion of some new sensational revelation in her voice. 'Big red and yellow job – one of them old-fashioned circus caravans, but we thought it might have something to do with the film. . .'

'Film?' shouted both children together. 'What film?'

'Oh didn't you know?' said Mrs Higgs with an air of surprise. 'Well, I should've thought you two would've known about it, being so thick with that Henry Partridge.'

'What's Henry got to do with it?' Lucy asked.

'Him and Billy Watt have done up this old traction engine, haven't they?' Mrs Higgs said. The children nodded. Billy Watt was the son of the farmer at Home Farm, and they knew that he and Henry had been restoring an old steam engine that Billy had discovered in one of his father's barns.

'Well there's this company coming to do a film in the Park, and they're getting all sorts of old engines and things for it,' Mrs Higgs continued, 'and old fairground stuff – all sorts of things, because it's about a circus or something. They're starting next week. They've hired a whole fair too – that one with the steam roundabout that goes round Chesham way every year.'

'What about the Steam Rally in the Park?' asked Martin. 'That's next week-end – will it still be on? That's what Henry and Billy were doing their engine for.'

'Oh that'll be on still,' Mrs Higgs assured them. 'Bigger and better I should think, on account of all them engines and things for the film being there.'

'It's twenty to nine,' said Mrs Lovell. 'If you two kids don't put a move on, you'll be late for school.'

After school that day Martin cycled up to the Folly to work on the model ship.

'Have you been burgled?' he asked rolling up his sleeves. 'Mrs Higgs said they had burglars at Billy's last night.'

'I know,' said Henry getting on with his own work. 'No one bothered us though. We did see a couple of rough-looking types hanging around yesterday afternoon, but they sloped off as soon as they realized they'd been spotted.'

'Do you think your things are safe here?' Martin said, thinking of the box.

'Who'd think there was anything worth breaking in for up here?' Henry countered.

'Someone might have watched you,' Martin suggested. Henry laughed.

'Don't worry, I don't keep much here these days. Sarah keeps most of the finished jobs at the shop,' he said. But of course that did not satisfy Martin, since it was not the models that he was worried about.

'Anyway,' said Henry, 'they didn't steal anything from Home Farm – pretty pointless really. Dad thought it might have been some kids with a grudge against old Watt.'

There was a pause while they both worked in silence.

'Have you heard about the film?' Martin asked casually.

'Oh yes,' said Henry equally casually, 'I'm in it.'

'You are?' exlaimed Martin, rather deflated, as he had hoped to tell Henry something he had not heard, but agog with curiosity nevertheless.

'Yes,' said Henry, 'the film company are hiring Lord Jim, and Billy and I are going along with him as extras.'

'What's it about?' Martin asked. Henry shrugged.

'I couldn't tell you,' he said. 'It all looks a bit rum to me. They're fetching in all this fairground and circus stuff, and the set they're building in the Park looks like a bit of a village. They've put it in that little valley at the far end – couple of cottages, village inn, bit of a castle for some reason, and a church up on the ridge. It all looks very ruined and romantic. Chap up there this morning said that it's all symbolical and something to do with dreams and illusions.' He laughed and added: 'I don't care what it's about so long as their money's real.'

Later, when discussing the matter with Lucy, Martin said:

'You know, we've been thinking of the Green Lady as a statue, but she probably won't be like that now, any more than the Fiddler is – and she's got people to help her, like Snowy's got us.'

'Well?' said Lucy. 'What about it?'

'Just this,' said Martin patiently, 'with all these people from the film and fair around, we won't notice strangers as much as we would normally, so it would be a good time for anyone to wander around the district looking for something, wouldn't it?'

6

THE STEAM FAIR

GORE HOUSE, the stately home to which the Park belonged, had long ago been turned into a school, and the Park itself was used now for grazing cattle, where it had not been ploughed up, but one could still see the old design of the landscape artist who had laid it out more than 200 years ago. The Park Woods were overgrown, trees fell in the Park and in the woods and were left where they fell, but once a year a little glory returned to Gore Park with the Steam Rally and Fete (proceeds donated to two charities for handicapped children), the biggest outdoor event of Dunsley's year, except when the Park accommodated the County Agricultural Show.

It was a glorious combination of steam-engine rally, fete, and all the traditional fun of the fair, with an amazing variety of inducements to roll up. If you tired of looking at huge, gleaming traction engines, you could go and listen to one of the steam organs which played continuously in various parts of the field. If that music was not quite to your taste, you could sit on the grass to listen to the band of the Irish guards and admire their gigantic wolfhound.

If you had money to spend, you could buy anything from a pot of home-made jam to a pair of brass candlesticks shaped like snakes and said to come from India, or you could try one of the innumerable ways of winning a teddy bear, a goldfish or a coconut. You might ride a donkey, a dodgem car, a chairplane, a swing boat, the Big Wheel, or a superb roundabout, which offered you a choice of gallant, galloping horses with flaring nostrils and flying manes, or fabulous birds possibly related to the peafowl.

If, finally, you felt yourself to be failing for hunger or thirst, there were vans selling hot dogs and hamburgers, candy floss and toffee apples, or tents offering tea and cakes, coffee and sandwiches, orange squash, lemonade and beer. The whole field was a roar of excitement from two in the afternoon to eleven at night, when the local by-laws insisted that the fair must close. Respectable ladies of the Women's Institute vied with raffish characters belonging to the fair for the custom of an unfailingly good-natured crowd. The sun shone, the band played, the steam whistles blew and everyone had the time of their lives.

On that Saturday morning Aunt Bea, a frequent visitor to Dunsley, arrived to stay for the week-end. She had promised to take a turn helping in the tea tent, and the moment she arrived she turned to and started to organize the Lovell family into a picnic.

'Whatever for?' said Dr Lovell plaintively. 'There'll be oceans of food and drink up there – Good heavens, Auntie, you're helping to dole it out yourself. Why take all this with us?'

'You don't want to have to stand around in queues all afternoon, do you?' said Aunt Bea reasonably.

'I don't want to go to a fete loaded up as if we were an expedition to find the source of the Nile either,' Dr Lovell muttered.

'That's all right,' said his father cheerfully, 'you take all the picnic things in the car, and Martin and I will escort the ladies across the fields.'

'Super,' said Dr Lovell unenthusiastically.

The whole family dressed up for the occasion. There was something flamboyant about the steam engines and the fair that encouraged one to wear the brightest clothes one had. Even Lucy, normally as indifferent to her appearance as Martin to his, wore her prettiest summer dress. Sarah joined them just as they left, having closed the shop for the afternoon, because everyone in the town would be buying things at the fete. She too was costumed to suit the day in a long dress all frilled and flounced and tucked, her coppery hair piled up on her head and puffed out at the sides in the style that was popular in Lord Jim's heyday.

'My dear, *what* a pretty dress!' Aunt Bea exclaimed. 'I don't think I've seen anything so nice since I was a child.'

The party moved off like a state procession: Grandfather with Mrs Lovell on one arm and Aunt Bea on the other in the lead, Sarah, Lucy and Martin bringing up the rear.

Henry and Billy with Lord Jim had already taken up their places in the rank of engines by the time the Lovell party arrived. Lord Jim was a huge black road locomotive, his massive form picked out with thin red and gold lines, his abundant brasswork polished to dazzling perfection. He was panting softly in the heat and his huge iron heart purred restfully. Henry and Billy had made a gallant attempt to live up to their monster's magnificence. They were wearing brilliant shirts, black waistcoats, top hats and luxuriant false whiskers. Billy looked particularly dramatic – his face red with the heat of the day and the engine, and framed by his own fair hair and some startling yellow whiskers, while the gorgeous colour scheme was completed by a purple shirt.

Sarah and everybody from No 28 walked round the three of them admiring without restraint, and then Billy sat up on the engine and Henry posed against one of Lord Jim's enormous driving wheels, his thumbs in the armholes of his waistcoat and a big cigar in his mouth, while Martin and Aunt Bea took photographs of them.

'Trying to look like Isambard Kingdom Brunel, I suppose,' said Sarah.

'Who's that?' Lucy asked.

'A great Victorian engineer,' Sarah told her, 'but I don't suppose he wore red shirts.'

After the Grand Parade of all the engines, and several events to test the drivers' skill, in which the iron monsters charged down the field at a smart walking pace, six at a time, weaving in and out of oil drums, Henry left Lord Jim to Billy and his girlfriend, and joined the Lovell party on its tour of the other attractions.

The fair had a curiously levelling effect on them all. Grandfather and Aunt Bea seemed to be transported back to the days and fairs of their youth, which compelled Dr and Mrs Lovell to be children again, and practically eliminated Sarah, Henry and the Lovell children from existence. They compromised with the situation by becoming, for that one afternoon, contemporaries at about the age of Lucy and Martin. Grandfather won a bowl of goldfish for Aunt Bea at the rifle range and a strange blue and white china dog for Mrs Lovell at the hoopla. Dr Lovell and Henry bowled unsuccessfully for a pig, which was, as they agreed after, a very good thing, as neither of them would have known what to do with the animal had they won it. They were more successful at the coconut shy, although Mrs Lovell said that a coconut was not really much more use to her than a pig, though admittedly less trouble.

When it was time for Aunt Bea to take her turn at serving tea, Grandfather decided to go with her.

'Well,' said Dr Lovell to the remainder of the party, 'what shall we infants do until the grown-ups are ready to give us our tea?'

'Rides!' shouted Lucy.

And so they rode: on the dodgems, on the Big Wheel and finally on the roundabout. Lucy and Martin chose a dapple grey horse and a black one side by side, Dr and Mrs Lovell were just behind them, and Sarah and Henry were a little way in front on two of the fabulous birds. Lucy was completely happy. Just for the moment all anxiety and the threatening shadow of the Lady disappeared. As she rode up and down and round and round, she imagined that they were all riding in a procession to a great feast. This was magic too, she thought, human magic that the Lady would steal if she could. Martin frowned sternly ahead, because although he had similar thoughts, *he* was riding into battle against the Lady and her allies.

Lucy turned round to wave to her parents and then leaned forward hoping that Sarah or Henry would turn round, so that she could wave to them too. It was then that she noticed the man just ahead of her and Martin. She wondered why she had not noticed him before, he was so oddly dressed – at least, what was odd about his clothes was really that they were so ordinary. On a day when everyone else seemed to have dressed up in their

brightest and most unusual summer clothes, he alone was wearing a dark suit, dark blue raincoat and a bowler hat. A raincoat on a day like this! thought Lucy, the poor man must be sweltering. He even had an umbrella, of all things. Perhaps he had heard a weather forecast for the wrong place. He did not look as if he were enjoying himself much either. He was a short, square man with a stodgy sort of face and a little moustache. He sat bolt upright on his horse, his umbrella held across the horse's neck, and stared in front of him at Henry and Sarah. Lucy felt she had seen him somewhere before.

The picnic was not nearly as bad as Henry had feared. He had not picnicked since he was a child, and all his memories of those occasions were more or less horrific, but this one, in keeping with the rest of the day, was entirely enjoyable. Henry was surprised, and not for the first time that day.

First he had been unpleasantly surprised to find that he would be sharing Sarah with the Lovell family, next he had been surprised to find that he was, nevertheless, enjoying himself. On several occasions in the past he had been irritated by the attention that Sarah paid to Lucy and Martin. They always seemed to be hanging around her, and she took all their games so seriously: that silly business with the white cat had been an especially annoying example of this sort of thing. He told himself that he was irritated, because Sarah ought to have grown out of nonsense like that, but really it was because he felt absurdly as if he were being excluded from something important. This afternoon, however, he found himself inside the same enchanted bubble of make-believe with them. Indeed it seemed to have expanded to take in the whole world. The fair, the engines, the crowds of people all belonged to the same magic existence that had been conjured up for him as a child by his grandfather's stories. The recollection of the old gentleman inspired him after tea to embark on an impromptu conjuring act.

He started by doing tricks with some lacy handkerchiefs he had bought from a charity stall.

'Are they your grandfather's tricks?' Martin asked, when Henry had finished and had given the handkerchiefs to the ladies with thanks for his tea.

'Of course they are!' Henry cried. 'The Great Alectoris rides again – for one night only!' and wrapping himself in a car rug which Aunt Bea had insisted on bringing in case the grass was damp, he launched into a fine dramatic performance. All manner of tea things found their way into his top hat, his handkerchief turned into a silk scarf which he gave to Sarah, Martin was found to have half a dozen marbles in his hair ('I shouldn't be surprised by anything you found in that haystack,' said his mother), and Lucy, it seemed, was very cruelly keeping a little china rabbit in her sandal. He finished by producing a miniature pack of playing cards, and doing some card tricks which all went hopelessly wrong and ended with the cards flying all over the place. When they were gathered up again, it was found that there were now two packs.

The party laughed and cheered and clapped. Grandfather repeatedly asked Aunt Bea if she didn't remember Henry's grandfather doing that trick at the Old Empire, and Mrs Lovell said she didn't understand why Henry couldn't solve his problem of what to do by going on the television.

The Lovell tribe were not the only people to be diverted by Henry's act. Another family group, who had also been picnicking nearby, were thoroughly enjoying the show, and on the steps of a big red and yellow horse-drawn caravan not far away sat a short, square man wearing a dark raincoat and a bowler hat, who watched and nodded, as if he too had seen the tricks before. Lucy noticed him again, and was once again teased by the feeling that she recognized him. She wondered vaguely if he were something to do with the fair, or the film perhaps, but she did not waste much thought on him while Henry was in action.

When the tea things were cleared away the party broke up. Sarah and Henry said they would go for a walk and wandered off in the direction of the woods, the older ones thought they would just stay where they were for a while, and Lucy and Martin decided to go across to the other side of the Park, to look round the film set. It was some distance away and the sounds of the fair, the steam organs and the band died away behind them, until they could hear only the occasional shriek of a steam whistle. They climbed the slope to the church, and surveyed the rest of the mock village.

'It would be quite a nice place to have a few houses, wouldn't it?' Lucy remarked.

'Mmm,' said Martin, 'it's a pity you can see they're not real – look, you can see the back of the castle wall from here.'

Lucy agreed that it was a pity and threw herself down on the grass.

'They couldn't possibly have all the buildings in the picture at once,' Martin went on sitting down beside her, 'because there isn't any place they could film from to get everything looking real – you can always see the back of something wherever you stand.'

'The inn looks real from here,' Lucy remarked idly.

As they were admiring the inn, Sarah and Henry emerged from the woods beyond it, and walked into the middle of the set. They were looking round and talking intently to each other. They went and sat down on the bench outside the inn.

'Better keep our heads down,' Martin suggested. 'Henry might not be pleased to see us just when he thinks he's got Sarah to himself.'

They grinned at each other and sprawled in the long grass by the churchyard wall, which looked solid and ancient enough, but sounded very wooden and hollow if you tapped it. Suddenly Martin raised his head and stared down into the valley.

'I say! Who's that?' he exclaimed.

'Sarah and Henry,' said Lucy, looking at him as if he had gone out of his mind.

'No, stupid, by the castle,' Martin said impatiently. 'He looks as if he's watching them.'

Lucy gasped and clutched her brother's arm.

'It's the man in the bowler hat,' she said, watching the dark figure by the castle.

'Who is he?' Martin asked again.

'I don't know,' said Lucy, 'but I've seen him twice today, and both times I think he was watching Sarah and Henry, or Henry anyway.' She told him about the other occasions when she had noticed the man in the bowler hat, but kept her uneasy feeling that she knew him to herself.

'He's definitely watching them now,' said Martin. 'Come on, let's go down and tell them.'

Henry was completely at his ease. He had Sarah's whole, undivided and flatteringly interested attention for everything he said, and he was taking the opportunity to tell her all about his latest plans for his future, which now looked a good deal more brilliant to him than it had when they first met. When he saw her eyes shift and stare past him, he felt suddenly deflated.

'What is it?' he asked. 'Not those two kids again?'

'No,' said Sarah, 'but I'm sure I saw *someone* standing over there by the castle. He ducked back as soon as I looked that way.'

'You're sure those children haven't followed us?' Henry said suspiciously.

'I don't think they'd do that,' said Sarah. 'Besides it was someone bigger than either of them and wearing dark clothes.'

'In that case I'll go and sort him out, whoever he is,' Henry said belligerently, and leaving his topper on the bench he marched towards the castle. He was not gone long and returned shaking his head.

'No one in sight,' he reported. 'I think you must have been seeing things. . .'

At that moment the children ran down the slope to them.

'Did you get him?' Martin demanded.

'Who?' said Henry. 'Did you see somebody?'

'There was a man watching you,' Lucy said and told them about the man with the bowler and his apparent interest in them. Sarah said:

'I knew there was someone there. I *felt* as if we were being watched. But why . . . ?'

'Well he's gone now,' Henry said, and then: 'What on earth's the matter?' for Sarah and the children were looking at each other anxiously.

'There's nothing very sinister about it,' Henry continued. 'Chap's been to the fete, decides as we all did to have a look at the film set – sees that Sarah has seen him, gets embarrassed and beats it, in case we think he's spying on us. No need to look so aghast about it.'

'But he *was* spying on you,' Martin insisted. 'Three times.'

'Coincidence,' said Henry.

But some of the shine had gone out of the day for all of them, and they made their way back to the fair in silence. On the way Lucy suddenly remembered where she had seen the man before. She drew Martin back.

'I *do* know who he is,' she whispered urgently. 'He was the man in the Magic Mountain at the toy fair, and I'm sure he's one of *hers*.'

7

THE MAN IN
THE BOWLER HAT

THE following morning it was Martin's turn to work at the Folly and keep watch on the box. The door was open when he arrived and he could see Henry standing by his bench, talking to a man wearing a dark raincoat and a bowler hat. His umbrella was leaning against the bench and he was examining the magic box. Henry was apparently demonstrating it to him.

'Fascinating,' the man murmured as Martin walked in, 'I don't think I've ever seen one quite like it before. I do wish you'd change your mind.'

'Sorry,' said Henry, 'but I couldn't think of selling it. Sentimental value, you know.'

'Pity,' said the man taking up his umbrella, 'it's just the thing I've been looking for.'

He turned to leave and had almost reached the door, before Martin saw to his surprise that he was carrying the box.

'Here, I say!' he exclaimed. Henry blinked and looked hard at the man, and then at the bench. A small attaché case was standing where the box had been a moment before.

'Hey!' Henry grabbed the case and strode to the door. 'I said no sale!' he said emphatically, relieving the man of the box and handing him his case.

'Good heavens!' said the man. 'What an extraordinary mistake to make.'

'Wasn't it just,' said Henry drily. He turned back to his bench frowning and replaced the box. He stared at it wondering how it could have looked, even for a moment, like an attaché case.

Martin lingered by the door for a moment, still not completely sure that it was in fact the same man – it was over a month since the toy fair and he had only seen the man by the castle from a distance – then he saw the man do something very odd. Although the sun was shining brightly, he started to open his umbrella as he walked down the slope. Halfway down he gave it a twirl and took off, his raincoat flapping slightly.

'Henry,' Martin called cautiously, 'come here and look, would you?'

But by the time Henry came to the door the man was no more than a flapping speck in the sky.

'Did you fetch me out to look at a crow,' he demanded ominously.

'I thought it looked bigger,' Martin said.

'Vulture? Eagle? Owl?' Henry suggested sarcastically.

As Martin followed Henry back to the bench he said:

'Who was that man?'

'Said he was an antique dealer. His speciality is apparently old fairground stuff and stage props. That's why he's here this week-end – interested in the fair. He knew about Grandpa and came along to see if I had any of his old stuff.'

'How did he know where to find you?'

'I expect he called at the farm and they told him where I'd be. Why?'

'Well,' said Martin carefully, 'that was the man who was following you yesterday.'

Henry stared at him.

'Are you suggesting,' he said, 'that Fly Fred there deliberately tracked me down for the sole purpose of nicking one of Grandpa's old props?'

'He did try to steal it, didn't he?' Martin pointed out, 'so he must've been pretty keen to get hold of it.'

'Why should he want it as much as that?' Henry murmured, polishing the box thoughtfully with his handkerchief.

'Granddad told us that conjurors keep their tricks secret, and sometimes pay a lot of money for a good one,' said Martin carefully. 'Perhaps this man wanted the box for a trick of his own.'

'Perhaps,' said Henry, 'and perhaps I'd better take a closer look at the old box. There may be something about it that I've missed. In the meantime. . .'

He put the box back on the top shelf of one of his cupboards and locked the door on it. He was quite sure of that: he definitely locked the door.

Martin left the Folly earlier than usual and pedalled hard all the way home, even down the long hill into the town. The gate into the archway was open, and so he rode straight in, shouted up the garden for Lucy in case she was in the orchard, propped his bicycle against the wall next to Sarah's gate and flung the gate open. He stopped short with surprise at the scene before him.

The garden table on the little patio behind the pottery was laid for lunch. Sarah and Lucy sat on folding chairs on one side of it, and on the other, on a wooden bench against the wall, sat Snowy and an elderly man, tall and thin, with long grey hair and a little pointed beard. He wore kneebreeches and a Norfolk jacket of grey tweed, and beside him on the bench lay a large dark cape and a hat with a low crown and broad brim. His clothes were well worn, but he had an air about him that was both grander and younger than he looked. A rucksack lay on the ground at his feet and beside it a violin case.

Snowy and the man looked round as the gate opened. Martin stared for a moment at the stranger and then at the violin case.

'Are you the Fiddler?' he asked.

The man laughed and bowed to him without rising from his seat.

'*The* Fiddler seems an overgenerous title,' he said. 'I can think

of a number I have known who deserve it better. There was
Paganini, for instance—'

'Name dropping!' muttered Snowy disgustedly, and Sarah
said:

'Martin this is my godfather, Mr Schwartz. Come and have
something to eat.'

The Fiddler pushed a third chair towards Martin with his foot. Snowy said:

'Yes, for goodness' sake come in and shut the gate. And stop gawping like that.'

Martin closed the gate and dropped into the chair.

'Wherever have you been?' he asked looking at the Fiddler curiously. He saw now that Mr Schwartz looked untidy and haggard, as if where he had been had not been too comfortable.

'I was about to explain when we heard your approach,' said the Fiddler. 'Snowy and I have only just arrived ourselves.'

'Sorry to interrupt,' Martin said politely. The Fiddler waved his apology aside.

'Now the story need only be told once,' he said, 'and anyway, you seemed to have some urgent news yourself. Perhaps we had better hear that first.'

Martin quickly told them about the attempt to steal the box, and when he had finished, Lucy added her account of the bowler-hatted man's behaviour of the previous afternoon, and her certainty that he was the man they had seen at the toy fair.

'Hang on a minute,' said Sarah. 'This bloke in the bowler hat may be a crook, but he doesn't *have* to be one of the Green Lady's henchmen. If he had a "magic" stand at the toy fair, his story might be true. He would know about Henry's grandfather if he was in the business himself – he could be nothing more than a dishonest collector.'

'But he *flew* away!' Martin nearly shouted with impatience.

'Oh yes,' said Sarah weakly. 'I'd forgotten that bit.'

'As it happens, I can confirm Martin's suspicions,' said the Fiddler. 'The same man, or his double, was one of the people who – er – delayed me. She's definitely on the move, she knows what she's after, and her agents are very active all of a sudden.'

He rubbed his head reflectively.

Sarah suddenly clapped a hand to her face.

'I've just remembered something,' she said. 'I was up at the farm last Wednesday, and Mrs Partridge was very cross because someone had been bothering her for old props of her father-in-law's. She said he was "some dealer chap" and he was very persistent and held her up for ages trying to get her to remember if there was any of the old conjuring stuff around still. She didn't say what he looked like or mention the box – perhaps she'd forgotten it. . .'

'But nevertheless, there was someone inquiring about the Great Alectoris's gadgets and it never occurred to you that there was anything in it to waste a second thought **on**,' said Snowy staring at her coldly. 'I thought you said you'd been keeping an eye on things.'

'I'm sorry, but what could we have done anyway?' Sarah demanded. 'We couldn't just pinch the thing.'

'You might have found some pretext for borrowing it, and then you could have hidden it,' said the cat. 'They might have thought it wasn't in these parts any more!'

'It's all very well telling me what I might have done,' Sarah said hotly, 'but why weren't you around to tell me at the time? You didn't even tell us *why* this box is so important.' She turned to the Fiddler. 'Don't you think we could have some explanations now? Snowy tells us that this Green Lady is plotting some sort of nastiness involving Henry's grandfather's box, and that we have to do something about it, but before I go a step further, I want to know what it's all about.'

'Very fair,' said the Fiddler, 'and if I had not been so persuasively detained you should have known much earlier.

'First a bit of history that you won't find in the history books – though you may still trace the outline of it in legends and fairy tales.

'In the early days, when humankind was beginning to emerge as the future rulers of the earth, this world was placed under what one might call a regency. The regents were natives of another world very close to this one – how should I put it? – so close that they overlapped. That's the nearest I can come to explaining it. It was quite easy then to move between that world and this.

'These Others were of an older race than humankind, and for the most part wiser (though not always as much *better* as they should have been, I'm afraid), and on the whole they managed things fairly well, although like most guardians, they could never believe that their charges were capable of doing anything by themselves.·

'Eventually, however, humankind began to grow up, to demand control over its own destiny, to look beyond the Old Gods for Truth's Very Self. At the same time, by some shift in the fabric of the universe, the two worlds began to slide round at an awkward angle to each other, so that passage between them became more difficult and the power which the Old Ones drew from their own world was weakened.

'At that point I suppose they should have retired gracefully to their own place, leaving humankind to take over its inheritance. Unfortunately things seldom go as smoothly as that, even in the best of families. There was a new spirit abroad in this world, and many of the Old Ones didn't understand it. The followers among humans of the new ways tended to be a bit too free with words like "superstition", "ignorance", "devils", and so forth, while the Old Ones often fought grimly to hang on to their old powers and privileges. At length it was clear that the only thing to do was to separate the two worlds completely. It was in any case increasingly difficult for them to maintain contact.

'The Old Ones were presented with a choice: either to withdraw to their own world or to remain in this, cut off from the power of the Other Side and retaining only whatever power they possessed in their own natures. Once the choice was made it could not be revoked. The Old Ones had to stay on which ever side they had chosen, because they could no longer cross back.

'But the worlds were not entirely sealed off from each other. There were four ways by which it was still possible to pass between them – four gates, as it were – the Earth Gate and the Water Gate which are controlled from this side, the Fire Gate and the Air Gate which are controlled from the Other. Though the Old Ones may not use them, these gates are open from time to time for humans and animals (now and then the Old Ones have beaten the ban by assuming animal form, but it's very risky). Captain Lovell went through the Water Gate, as Sarah did when Snowy took her to see the Captain and the mice.'

'Just a minute,' said Sarah. 'How do *you* know all this – Uncle William Schwartz?' The Fiddler smiled and Snowy said:

'How do you think he knows, for goodness' sake?'

'You mean *he's* one of the Old Ones?' Lucy exclaimed.

'I'm afraid so,' said the Fiddler. 'Snowy too. He keeps the Water Gate, I the Earth Gate. We stayed, as others did, because we felt that there was still a job for us here – or just because we liked it.

'The greatest of the Old Ones withdrew – most of them. They were lords in their own place and few of them saw any reason why they should stay here and be less. There were others, however, who had grown accustomed to being much more highly respected Here than they could hope to be on the Other Side, and so they stayed, thinking they'd be all the more important when their greater colleagues had gone. They didn't understand that they were respected only for the power that would no longer be available to them. Some, who could expect to be as well off on one side as the other, chose on the flip of a coin, or left the choice to make itself, being content to stay wherever they happened to be when the frontier closed.

'The smaller folk who stayed found that not much changed for them. They went on helping or hindering the humans they lived alongside, much as they always had. Those of us who had read the signs aright, however, knew that if we wanted to continue to take an active part in the affairs of this world, we should have to make some kind of terms with the new spirit that worked in it. Many became as good Christians as ever went to church o' Sundays, and not a soul would ever have known them from their human neighbours.

'But for those who stayed in the belief that they'd still rule Here, there came a rude awakening. They were very angry to discover that they didn't add up to much in this world once they'd lost touch with the Other.

'Our friend the Green Lady was one of these. In her pride, she had believed that nothing could shake her power, and she grew bitter and resentful towards humankind when she found that they no longer cared two pins for her. She refused to exercise any of her remaining influence for the good of the people among whom she lived, and she determined that if ever she could be revenged on them for slighting her, she would.

'I found her in Captain Lovell's home by chance. I was in this district on other business, but since an important part of my job at any time is keeping an eye on the Old Ones who stayed on, I thought I had better hang around and find out how she was behaving. I saw that she was bent on mischief right away, and she was suspiciously interested in Snowy's friends the boggart and the dryad: I don't think she'd realized that there were still quite a few of the Old Ones Here, and I imagine she has drawn some of the discontented elements into her plot. However, I thought it would be enough to put a stop to what she was doing there and then – make her look foolish, so that no one would take her seriously in the future. I should have taken her more seriously myself.'

'I don't think you're quite fair to yourself,' Snowy said, rather to the children's surprise. 'I think we might have kept her under control easily enough if she hadn't come across that infernal box.'

'Yes, what about the box?' said Sarah. 'Where does that fit into all this?'

'I wish we really knew that,' said the Fiddler ruefully. 'It isn't one of the Gates but it *is* a way of getting to the Other Side. And that ought to be impossible. I think it must have been made by some magician long ago when it was easier to cross.'

'It was the mice that first realized that there was more to it than anyone had guessed,' Snowy said, taking up the story. 'They found that occasionally when the back of the box opened to let them out, it opened on a place they didn't recognize – and not always the same place either. Sometimes it was a forest, sometimes sea, sometimes just a swirling fog. Any mouse that went out on those occasions was never seen again. When the Great Alectoris got the Green Lady, he used her in one of his tricks with the box, and she must have seen that Other Place, guessed that it was her old home, and started scheming to draw power from There to take her revenge on humans.

'I met the mice about the time the conjuror retired. They told me about the place through the box, and about the Lady. They didn't know what would become of them next, and so I suggested that they should go through the box to the Other Side and stay there as frontier guards. Captain Lovell was already occupying a similar post in another part of the border country.

'When the Lady disappeared I suppose we should have done something about the box – but unfortunately we left it for some more convenient time that never came.'

Martin had been frowning and now he said:

'I don't understand – she's bigger than the box, so how could she have gone in it?'

'How do you know how big she is, or was, or how big the box was?' Snowy said. 'She may have been bigger when you saw her than she was then. Or the box may be smaller now. Neither are quite what you'd expect after all.'

'But what's this awful thing she's going to do?' Sarah asked. 'How will it help her to go back to the Other Side?'

'She can't do that,' said the Fiddler. 'Snowy can cross because of his animal shape, but she can't – and she doesn't need to. She only has to send some human to steal for her the Tokens in which a great part of the power of the Other Side is locked.'

'What are the Tokens?' Martin asked.

'A spear and a cauldron,' said Snowy, the hair rising along his back. 'And they must never fall into her hands. Their power must never be loosed in this world.'

'It's to prevent that, that we are asking for your help,' the Fiddler concluded.

'Would they enable her to drain people and things more quickly?' Sarah said.

'More than that,' said the Fiddler. 'Normally Snowy and I would be more than a match for her (he was off guard when she stuck him to the jug – she couldn't have done it otherwise). But if she had the Tokens she could turn against us the full power of our own world and our own kind, and we should be helpless.'

'We can't very well *not* help, can we?' Lucy said.

'It may be dangerous,' the Fiddler warned. 'Look at Snowy and think what she might do to you.'

'Sounds as if it would be just as bad if she had everything her own way,' said Martin.

'I agree – we're bound to do anything we can,' said Sarah, 'but it would have been so much easier if you had come when you said you would, before she escaped from the museum.'

The Fiddler smiled wryly.

'Yes. I'm afraid I underestimated her again,' he said. 'I thought I could pick up some information if I came into the district quietly on foot. I also wanted to contact someone on the Other Side – it was the first of May, remember, and May Eve is one of the best times for getting messages through. My "line" as you might call it has been very unreliable for a long time, and I wanted to give myself the best possible chance of connecting. However, it didn't work (which is something else for us to worry about, by the way), and so I pitched my tent and settled down for an hour or two of sleep, before meeting Sarah.

'I'd hardly dozed off, when the tent collapsed on top of me. I thought one of the donkeys I'd seen tethered a little way off must have broken loose and wandered into the tent in the dark. Then I felt something moving over me, feeling my shape under the canvas. Then someone hit me on the head. When I came to I was lying tied up in a bunk in a caravan. There were two people there, but I never saw them properly, and they must have kept me drugged or spellbound, because I had no idea how long I was there, until I woke up this morning, tied and gagged, to the sound of a terrific mewing outside. I heard a man's voice say, "Been locked out then Puss?" and the door opened a bit to let Snowy in and then closed again.

'In no time at all he had done a splendid job of chewing through the string that tied my hands, and I was able to manage the rest myself. My rucksack had been searched but nothing had been taken, and my fiddle was undamaged, so we just walked out. Then I discovered that I'd been imprisoned in a red and yellow showman's caravan, which was standing on the edge of a fair in the Park. We waited around discreetly just long enough to see your friend with the bowler hat come back to the caravan. When he came out again a minute later he looked so flustered that we knew he must have been one of the people who had been keeping me there. Then we came here.'

'And why haven't you been around?' Sarah asked Snowy. 'Nobody kidnapped you.'

'I have been simply unable to move,' said the white cat bitterly. 'I imagine that the Lady's current activity is reinforcing the original spell. Or else it's because she's somewhere near at hand. I can't think why it slackened off today.'

'Could there be someone else working on our side?' Martin suggested hopefully. The Fiddler shook his head doubtfully.

'There *is* someone in these parts who might have found out that something was afoot, and decided to toss an independent spanner in the works, just for the sake of a bit of mischief,' he said. 'But it's not someone we could possibly rely on for regular assistance – just as likely to turn on us next if we did.'

'So what happens next?' Sarah asked.

'Frankly it's difficult to say,' the Fiddler replied. 'We have to dispose of the box and stop the Lady for good – but I need help from the Other Side. I must have some support from the Warden of the Marches, and as I said I just haven't been able to get in touch with him.'

'Can't Snowy go and find him?' Sarah asked. 'Or one of us even?'

'No,' said the Fiddler firmly, 'we're in the wrong phase of the worlds.' He picked up a magazine from the seat beside him. 'The two worlds are set at an angle to each other in time and space,' he explained. 'Look, hold this picture so that you're looking at it from the side. It distorts it you see, makes the figures look narrower. That's what happens when you look at the time of one world from the other. Only both worlds are moving – *through* each other – all the time, and the distortion is changing all the time, so that sometimes the time on the Other Side seems shorter than ours and sometimes longer. At the moment it's longer – an hour would seem like several days. We can't afford the time, or for that matter the risk of you getting caught in a time trap.'

'There is a way,' said Snowy quietly.

'Only as a last resort,' said the Fiddler.

'But we *must*,' Snowy insisted. 'The almanack isn't detailed enough to tell us how the box works, neither of us can work it out from the tables, so—'

'What sort of tables do you mean?' Martin asked. The Fiddler produced from an inside pocket a small booklet with a thick grey paper cover, on which was printed:

JEROME'S SPACE–TIME TABLES
Including Jerome's Theory of Precession
and Sylvester's Equations

He handed it to Martin. It was full of very complicated mathematics and a sort of time table linking certain times of certain days with map references. Martin and Lucy looked at it blankly, but something about the title rang a bell in Lucy's memory. Suddenly she knew what it was.

'Weren't the conjuror's mice called Jerome and Sylvester?' she asked. 'Were they named after these people?'

'Well done,' said the Fiddler. 'Actually they *are* these people. They were always very intelligent and ingenious creatures, and their removal to the Other Side made them even more so. They have studied the relationships between the two worlds in time and space, and worked everything out mathematically. It used to be rather hit and miss and awful things happened from time to time – like when Oisin, the grandson of Finn MacCool, married a princess from the Other Side and stayed there three years, then wanted to visit his home again. But he crossed both ways at the wrong times, and found that he'd been gone for three *hundred* years, and could never get back. That sort of thing can't happen now, because we can just look up the best time and place and Gate to use and cross with the minimum of fuss – those of us who may, that is.'

'All very well,' said Snowy fidgeting irritably, 'but as I see it we need Jerome to calculate how to get rid of the Lady and the box, and the Warden to provide the power to do it, and at the moment we can't contact either through the normal channels. It would be quite safe to send—'

'We can't do anything until tomorrow anyway,' said the Fiddler quickly, 'and then if nothing has come through, we'll see.'

'Whatever you do, I think I'll try to persuade Henry to let me keep the box for a while,' said Sarah. 'I'm going up to the Folly tomorrow afternoon to fetch some models and perhaps he'll let me borrow it then.'

'Tomorrow, tomorrow,' said Snowy impatiently. 'Anything could happen before then.'

8

HENRY'S CURIOUS ADVENTURE

AFTER Martin left the Folly, Henry worked on alone for a while. He was strangely uneasy, and it took all the common sense he supposed himself to possess to persuade himself that there was nothing to feel uneasy about. The unusual atmosphere of the day before seemed to have made him more sensitive to suggestions he would previously have dismissed out of hand, so that he had been unaccountably disturbed by the thought of someone following Sarah and himself in the Park. The attempt to steal the box was nothing in itself, but Martin's assertion that the would-be thief was the same man who had been watching them, not to mention his peculiar behaviour over that crow, was rather unsettling. The more so since Henry, though he would never have confessed it, was not sure that it *had* been a bird Martin had shown him. Of course it had to be a bird, because there was nothing else it could have been – but that thought was not somehow as comforting as it should have been to a sensible, practical person.

As he tidied up his workroom before going home for lunch he made a great effort to push all the nonsense out of his head. Nonsense, that was what it was, all of a piece with talking cats. Good heavens, if he started letting himself see dark mysteries in a dishonest collector and an unfamiliar bird, it would not be long before he was completely round the bend. All the same . . . he looked round the room at his models and tools. There was quite a bit of stuff here now, some of it well worth stealing. He put everything of value out of sight and locked the door of the tower behind him when he left. He was quite sure of that.

At lunch Henry mentioned the man who had tried to buy the magic box, and he was working the incident up into a good story, when his mother broke in on him.

'There!' she exclaimed. 'That'll be the same chap that was round here last week pestering me for some of your grandfather's old stuff.'

Henry was surprised, but when his mother proceeded to describe the man exactly, he was rather more than surprised, he was suddenly and reasonably oppressed by a feeling that something very odd and sinister was going on.

' . . . I don't know what there was about him,' Mrs Partridge concluded, 'but I just didn't like the look of him at all. He was very polite and all that, but there was something wrong.'

'You'd better be careful with all those bits and pieces of yours,' Mr Partridge said. 'You don't want to lose stuff you've spent so much time on.'

Henry stared at his father. Since it was not so long ago that Mr Partridge had said that he was fed up with seeing a son of his fiddling around with toy trains, when he ought to be getting down to something serious, this suggestion that the things Henry made were worth looking after represented a considerable change of heart.

'Knick-knackeries?' Henry murmured. Mr Partridge contrived a hearty laugh.

'Well now,' he said, 'I wasn't to know there was any living in that kind of thing, was I? But if that young woman of yours can make a business out of her pots, I suppose your bits could fetch a decent price too.'

Henry glowered.

'They do, as a matter of fact,' he said. 'As a further matter of fact, they turn out to be catching on so much that Billy Watt is probably going to come in with me on it. And there's this film – that could be an opening for us if we use it properly.

'I must say,' he continued resentfully, 'it's a fine thing if it takes some scatty girl to convince you that your son isn't completely wasting his time.'

Mr Partridge winked knowingly at his wife.

'Scatty girl, eh?' he said.

Henry rose from the table, but his resentment lacked conviction. 'That young woman of yours' stuck too agreeably in his mind for him to feel other than amiable. At the kitchen door he turned and said cheerfully:

'Pottery isn't very respectable, you know – all arty-crafty and knick-knackery.'

'Sarah's a very nice girl,' his mother remarked complacently to his departing back.

'He could go further and fare worse,' her husband agreed.

Before Henry could return to the Folly that afternoon he had some work to do on a tractor. The job did not take too long and there was nothing that urgently required attention in his workshop, yet he found himself feeling extremely anxious to get back. It was about four o'clock when he was able to return to the tower.

As he approached the Folly he thought that Sarah must be there, for the door was open and she was the only person besides himself who had a key. But he had not been expecting her, and if she had come to the Folly and found him not there, she would certainly have made her way to the farm.

The workshop was dark after the bright sunlight outside, strangely chilly too, and it was a few seconds before Henry realized that there *was* someone there, but it was not Sarah.

A woman was seated on his work bench: the most strikingly handsome woman Henry had ever seen. He could not have said whether she was young or old – she had a peculiarly ageless look. She was wearing a long green dress, with a high neck and full sleeves, and on her head a close fitting cap, covered with green stones. Her skin was smooth and pale, but her hair was black and shone with the greenish iridescence of a crow's wing. Her mouth was made up with startlingly red lipstick and her fingernails were varnished with the same vivid colour. Henry stood and stared at her. She looked not quite real, and in her hands she held his grandfather's magic box.

'How did you get in?' he said blankly.

The woman threw back her head, mainly it seemed to show off her long, white neck, and laughed, displaying to the best effect her white teeth. Toothpaste advertisement smile, Henry thought, phoney.

'I flew down the chimney!' she cried, opening her eyes very wide at him.

Henry was completely at a loss and beginning to feel oddly uncomfortable.

'No chimney,' he remarked vaguely. The woman pouted with conscious charm.

'Spoilsport,' she said, 'all right, I just walked in at the door.'

'That's the point,' said Henry, pulling himself together. 'I thought I'd locked it.'

He examined the lock briefly, but it showed no signs of having been forced.

'Well if you did, someone else unlocked it,' the woman said reasonably, turning her attention back to the box. 'Tell me about this thing.'

'Ah!' Henry exclaimed, remembering the other thing that was wrong. 'How did you get that?'

'It was just standing there,' his visitor said innocently. She slid off the bench and placed the box in exactly the place where it had stood that morning when the man in the bowler hat had examined it. 'Right there,' she repeated, moving it half an inch to the right and smiling brilliantly at him over her shoulder.

Henry moved uneasily across to the bench and inspected the box. He knew he had locked the Folly when he went for lunch, he always did, and he had locked the box in the cupboard as soon as the man in the bowler hat had gone. He was sure. . . The box seemed to be exactly the same as usual. It was undamaged and everything was in working order. Absentmindedly he showed the woman the revolving compartments and told her about the striped mice, while he racked his brains for an explanation.

'This is quite fascinating,' said the woman. 'You must let me show you why I was so interested in it.'

'Look,' said Henry putting the box down on the bench, 'I don't want to seem rude, but this is private property and I keep a few things here, so you see I'm a bit concerned to find that doors I thought I'd locked have been opened, and things I thought I'd put away are standing around for anyone to pick up. . .'

The woman stepped quickly away from the bench, putting her hands behind her back and biting her lip childishly. Henry was less charmed than irritated.

'All right,' he said, 'I'm not suggesting that you broke in and burgled my workshop, but you must see how it is, surely? I'd like to know how you came to be here, in case someone else has been up to something.'

He was thinking of the man with the bowler hat, and wondering if there might be something more than fancy to what he had been feeling. The woman returned to the bench and started playing with the box. Henry observed that she knew exactly how to work it: very quick, he thought.

'Actually there's nothing much to tell you,' she said. 'I missed my way somehow, and when I saw your tower I thought I'd found the set. Of course when I got right up to it I could see it was real, but the door was open a bit, and so I peeked in, and there was this box, so I was sure the place must have something to do with us. I thought I'd better stay here until someone came.'

'Do you mean you're something to do with the film?' Henry asked.

'That's right, something to do with the film,' she said, smiling indulgently in a way that made Henry feel quite sure that she was somebody famous whom he should have recognized. He blushed but floundered on.

'Well why did that box make you think this place was connected with the set?'

'Oh, I'd rather *show* you!' she exclaimed, flinging her arms open in a dramatic gesture. 'Follow me!'

She walked past Henry to the door, where she stopped and looked at him over her shoulder. Henry knew once again that he was meant to be charmed, and that once again irritated him a little. It also amused him a little, none of which prevented him from being interested a lot.

'Be with you in a minute,' he said. He replaced the box in the cupboard, locked the door once more, and when he had followed his visitor out, he carefully locked the door of the Folly, trying it afterwards to see that it was fast.

'You *are* cautious,' the woman remarked with some amusement.

'My life's work,' Henry murmured.

When they reached the road on the other side of the hill, where the woman said she had left her car, Henry's suspicions and his vague unease about her vanished in delight. There before him stood the most beautiful old car he had ever seen, its green paint, enormous brass headlamps and high leather covered seats as fresh and clean as on the day some sixty years ago when it had first taken the road. It was almost too perfect.

'Is it genuine?' Henry said.

'Oh yes,' said the lady, 'it was quite a business getting him restored, but he's a real veteran.'

Henry examined the car lovingly, while the lady watched him with a look of amusement.

'I thought you'd like Oscar,' she said, 'I saw those little engines when you opened your cupboard, and I knew you'd be the sort of person who'd fall for him.'

She climbed up into the driving seat.

'Come on,' she said.

Henry stared for a second. He had forgotten why he had come with her.

'The box,' she reminded him, 'if you can show me where the set is, I can show you why your box interested me so much.'

While Henry cranked the engine she wound a long green scarf round her head and shoulders. When he climbed up beside her, she showed her teeth in another brilliant smile. Henry wondered why she seemed so amused all the time. Was there

something funny about him? He decided in the end that it was just an actressy affectation to take any opportunity to smile. He had never been personally acquainted with a film star before, but he remembered the leading lady of a student drama group, for which he had once been stage manager, and she had put on some very strange manners at times. He supposed it must be the inevitable result of constantly pretending to be someone else.

What with his reflections about actresses, and the woman's continuous flow of talk about the car (which was interesting) and the film (which was incomprehensible), it seemed to Henry that they came in no time at all to the place where the Park Woods ran right down to the road, and he wondered whether a car as old as Oscar was supposed to be could possibly travel so quickly. He made some jocular remark to that effect and his companion pouted as she pulled in to the side of the road.

'You're not a gentleman,' she complained. 'Anyone else would have paid tribute to my fascinating company, instead of doubting the genuineness of my car!'

Henry apologized. To his surprise she stopped the engine.

'It's all right,' she said, before he could speak, 'I know where we are now. I must have come down the wrong lane, wouldn't you say so?'

Henry did not remark, as he certainly would have done to Sarah, that he could not possibly know if she had taken the wrong road, unless he knew where she had come from. He just smiled and said he supposed so. The shaking of the car and her constant smile had begun to confuse him again.

'But the set is further on,' he said.

'Not the bit I want to show you,' she insisted.

Henry dismounted and helped her down. She led him into the wood.

Not far from the road the ground sloped steeply upwards. A large part of the hillside had been dug away in quarrying the chalk years ago, and the woman led the way to the top of this low cliff by a faint path, which Henry might not have noticed himself. He thought he caught a glimpse of a building beyond the trees, and it occurred to him that if that were part of the film set, it was situated in a particularly awkward spot for filming. He had just started to say:

'I shouldn't have thought the light would be very good here...'

But then they emerged into a clearing a few yards from the edge of the chalkpit, and Henry was silenced again.

The structure that stood before him was not, as he had supposed, one of the film company's mock houses: it was his grandfather's box.

Of course that was nonsense. It was not the box – it was a man-sized replica of it, identical in every detail. Henry would almost have been ready to swear that not only was the carving and gilding the same, but even the chips and stains had been reproduced. He stared at the box and then turned speechless to the woman.

'You see?' she cried triumphantly. 'You see what I mean?'

'How on earth. . . ?' Henry shook his head in wonder. 'Why?' he said.

'I couldn't say,' the woman said shrugging her shoulders. 'I mean the whole thing's one big bamboozle from start to finish, so a gadget like this is quite in keeping.'

Henry supposed she must be talking about the film, but she might as well have meant that afternoon, for he was as thoroughly bamboozled as he had ever been in his life. The woman produced a cigarette case and a long green cigarette holder. She offered him a cigarette.

'No thanks, I don't,' he said vaguely.

She took a cigarette herself and fitted it into the holder. Henry fumbled in his pocket for a box of matches and lit the cigarette for her. It was black and smelt very peculiar. The match flared and spluttered slightly as Henry held it out.

Once her cigarette was alight, the woman turned her attention back to the giant box.

'I think you might find the inside as interesting as the outside,' she said. 'I found out about it the other day, when I was searching for some things that must have been left somewhere round here. It was quite a puzzle to me.'

Henry was now feeling more than confused: suddenly he felt quite dizzy. The green, curling smoke of the cigarette seemed to be everywhere, twisting in the sunlight of the clearing, and its heavy, sweet smell was almost more than he could stand.

'Really?' he said weakly. He was hardly listening to what she was saying, because all his attention was taken up by his efforts to conceal his sudden faintness.

'Yes,' she went on, as if she had noticed nothing. 'I'm not even sure now whether the things I was looking for were there or not. I might easily have missed them.'

'What was that?' Henry said, trying to keep up with what she was saying.

'A sort of cauldron thing and a spear – nothing much you know, but you have to have the same things all the time – can't be seen walking up to a door with one sort of pot, and then walking out on the other side in the next shot with a completely different one!'

She went on talking and laughing, while Henry tried to concentrate on what she was saying, but the dizziness was worsening and the smoke seemed to become more overpowering every minute.

'Very strange,' he murmured at random, as if replying to something she had said.

' . . . Well, perhaps you might?'

The words seemed to pop suddenly out of a kind of haze. Henry started.

'I said, since you know about these things, perhaps you might like to see for yourself. The inside, I mean.' She raised her eyebrows.

Henry turned to the box. The front was now open and he gathered that he was being invited to inspect it. Still dazed and feeling slightly sick, he stepped into the box. It seemed to lurch. Something clicked behind him and he was suddenly in darkness. The box lurched again, throwing him against the side, and he leaned there for a few seconds while everything rocked. When the inside of the box was still again, he found that his head was clearer, although he now felt giddy from the movement, and he supposed he must have been affected by the cigarette smoke, though he could not imagine what could have been in it to make him feel so ill.

Henry felt round the sides of the compartment he was in. It was like a big drum, exactly like the inner compartments of his grandfather's box, but man-sized instead of mouse-sized. Right, he thought, if it's exactly the same, it should turn a bit further and let one out at the back. He chuckled to himself: yes, this would be quite a puzzle to anyone who didn't know the trick of it, and it would certainly be easy to overlook something left in one of the compartments. For a second he felt dizzy and confused again, but it passed as he continued to examine the compartment as well as he could by touch. It really did need two to work it, he thought. Of course it was as easy to make a vanishing box for people as for mice, though he would have thought it would be just as well to have some way of working it from the inside. He felt round again, and experienced a moment of panic when he could feel nothing but smooth walls.

'Turn it a bit further,' he shouted, hoping he sounded cheerful. 'I'm not at the back yet.'

There was no reply. The panic flickered again. Poor old mouse, thought Henry. Before shouting again, he crouched down and felt round the floor. Either because he had touched something which operated the mechanism, or because someone outside had set the thing in motion again, the drum jolted once more and tipped him suddenly out on to the grass.

Henry picked himself up and looked at the box. He had been let out at the back, just like the mice. The inner compartments of the box were still revolving slowly, and he watched as the rear exit closed invisibly. Smiling appreciatively he walked round the box to discuss its workings and how they could check whether all the compartments were empty. Possibly the lady was not aware of some of the manoeuvres of which the ingenious machinery was capable.

However, the woman in green was not in front of the box, nor anywhere in sight. Even more strange, the smell of her cigarette smoke, which had hung so heavily in the clearing a few moments ago, had completely gone too.

'What the devil is she playing at?' he muttered to himself.

He turned to the path by which they had entered the clearing, intending to return to the edge of the chalkpit, to see if her car was still on the road. He could not see why she should strand him there, but her behaviour was altogether rather unaccountable. He had been walking several minutes, when he realized that he should have come to the cliff within as many seconds. He shook his head. Must still be muzzy, come the wrong way, he thought.

It took a little longer for him to discover that if he hoped to find the road, there was no right way, for there was no road. On one side he found that the wood thinned and was succeeded by totally unfamiliar downland, on the other it seemed to go on indefinitely. In fact, it was not the woman who had disappeared, but himself, for he was certainly not in the same place as he had been when he stepped into the box. Indeed, he was in no place he had ever seen before. He walked slowly back to the box and sat down beside it to consider his situation very carefully.

9

SKIRMISH IN THE WOODS

The party at Sarah's continued to discuss their possible courses of action after lunch, but although they went over the same ground again and again, they were no nearer to deciding anything definite and only became more edgy. Snowy continued to insist on immediate action, while the Fiddler tried to calm them all down. Eventually, shortly before four o'clock, Sarah stood up and said:

'I agree with Snowy; I think we ought to do something now.'

Snowy pricked his ears.

'And what has brought you over to my side, I wonder?' he said.

'I've been thinking while we've been going through all this,' she said. 'They've been in the district for several weeks now, since they picked up Uncle William. Ten days ago they went in for a spot of burglary. Now they've located the box definitely – I don't think we can hang about a moment longer, because I don't think they will.'

'Burglary ten days ago?' said Snowy sharply. 'What's this?'

Lucy and Martin told him about the raids on The Yews and Home Farm.

'And why do you think those must have been the work of the Lady's agents?' the cat demanded. Sarah shrugged.

'A farm on the edge of Dunsley and the house where Captain Lovell used to live,' she said. 'The wrong farm and the wrong Lovell house, as it happened, but if the burglars *weren't* the Lady's agents looking for a magic box and a china cat, what were they? Not the ordinary sort of criminal, because they didn't take anything.'

'Very well,' said the Fidder, 'we'll go and get the box. I'm sorry to have delayed things so long.'

When they arrived at the Folly it was clear that they were too late. The door was open as were the two cupboards inside, but of Henry and the box there was no sign. Martin returned to the door and looked up into the sky. In a moment he had spotted what he was looking for.

'There he is!' he shouted.

The others joined him. The flapping object did not look like a bird, but it did not look like anything else really – unless you were looking for a man in a bowler hat and loose raincoat, flying through the air under a twirling umbrella.

'He's going down behind those trees,' said Lucy. 'Where will he land?'

'If he really is landing it would be somewhere at the top of the Park Woods,' said Sarah, 'but it might be a trick.'

'Let's go after him and see,' said Martin at once.

They drove away from the Folly towards the Park Woods in a tense silence, ready to quarrel with each other if they could not find the people they really wanted to quarrel with. It was impossible to drive straight to the place where they thought the man might have landed, because there was no direct road, and they were obliged to take a roundabout route along narrow twisting lanes.

'Are you sure this is the quickest way?' Martin asked anxiously.

'Quite sure,' Sarah snapped back, 'unless you think we should take to the fields. Or sprout wings and fly perhaps?'

Martin subsided for a moment, then thought of something else.

'Oughtn't we to have told Henry?'

Sarah did not reply, and Martin was about to repeat his question when Lucy said:

'Oh Sarah! You don't think they've got Henry too, do you?'

'Why not?' said Sarah. 'He was supposed to be spending this afternoon at the Folly, but he *wasn't* there. And don't forget it isn't only the box she needs, she wants someone to go through it for the Tokens.'

'But Henry couldn't get into that box,' Martin objected.

'It might not be as difficult as you think,' Snowy said.

As they turned into the lane that ran through the top of the Park Woods, Sarah slowed down.

'Now,' she said, 'whereabouts do you reckon he would have come down, if he was landing when we saw him?'

'Somewhere near the old chalkpit,' said Martin at once, for he had been thinking about it since they left the Folly. 'It's on the right, a little way down this lane.'

'Well, keep your eyes peeled everyone,' said Sarah. 'I'll drive slowly to the end of this stretch of the woods, and then if—'

'I say! Look at that super car!' exclaimed Martin.

Sarah glanced at the green veteran car standing on the opposite verge, and then braked sharply and swung the van across to park in front of it.

'If old cars fascinate you so much, why don't we all go down to Beaulieu one day—' Snowy began.

'It's not the car that interests me,' Sarah said flinging open the door of the van and jumping out. 'It's Henry's jacket!'

She ran to the old car and grabbed the jacket that was lying on the seat. It was pale blue with fine red stripes and was unmistakably Henry's. The others joined her.

'I'd say we could start looking here,' she said.

'Up there,' said the Fiddler turning towards the chalkpit. 'Don't you think so Snowy?'

But Snowy was no longer with them. The Fiddler looked grave.

'Yes, she's up there,' he said. 'It's no use looking for Snowy now. I'm afraid we shall have to manage this without him.'

He led Sarah and the children to the path by which Henry and the woman in green had ascended to the top of the chalkpit not so long before.

They understood at once why the Fiddler was so sure that this was the right place to look for the Green Lady. The air seemed to thicken against them the moment they set foot on the path. The ground seemed to be stretching under their feet, for although they took normal steps they were covering the distance at a snail's pace. They became aware of a strange smell too, faint at first but quickly strengthening until it threatened to choke them – a sweet, sickly smell carried on a faint greenish smoke. It was first cold and then, as they came under the trees, unbearably hot.

'We're not getting anywhere,' Martin gasped when they had managed to climb a yard or so up the path. The Fiddler stopped, mopping his forehead.

'We must put out all the strength we have against her,' he said. 'We shall miss Snowy, but we must try.'

To the surprise of the others he produced a violin and a bow from one of the capacious pockets of his old-fashioned jacket (quite a conventional violin, Martin noticed, remembering Snowy's story). He folded his handkerchief into a pad and tucked it and the violin under his chin.

'Think of the best things you know,' he said, 'fresh air, sunshine, running about with no shoes on, making things – anything that makes you happy.'

He struck up a brilliant, jigging tune, and at once the thick, rotting air gave back a little. They all moved forward at a natural pace, concentrating as hard as they could on pleasant thoughts, but soon the sickening smell daunted them again.

'Sing!' commanded the Fiddler. He played an elaborate flourish and started on the Agincourt Carol. The children knew some of it, because they had been learning it at school. They hesitated, but Sarah started singing at once as loudly as she could:

'Our King went forth to Normandy. . .'

Lucy and Martin joined in at the second line. Their three voices sounded flat and muffled at first, but as they moved slowly, but steadily now, up the path, the heavy atmosphere gave way before them step by step, and their voices rang clearer and truer. The song swept them forward and they forgot everything else. As they went on they became aware, at the edges of their minds – rather as one catches sight of an indistinct movement out of the corner of one's eye – of other voices joining theirs, many other voices. As well as the violin they seemed to hear husky reeds, shrill trumpets and urgent rattling drums, faster and more urgent every moment, until the whole wood was pounding with the triumphant rhythm, until the four of them strode into the clearing on a blare of sunlight, as if they were indeed marching at the head of all the grace and might of chivalry.

Everything came to a shattering halt, and there was silence in the empty clearing, silence and sunlight dodging between the leaves of the beech trees all round.

'What's happened?' said Lucy, half dazed.

'She's gone,' said Martin.

'Yes,' said the Fiddler.

'We beat her,' said Martin. 'We drove her away.'

'Yes,' said the Fiddler wearily. He put the violin back in his pocket, shook out his handkerchief and mopped his face again.

'But there's nothing . . .' Lucy began.

'Not quite nothing,' Sarah exclaimed, darting across the clearing. Something was lying at the foot of a tree on the other side – a box, the Conjuror's box, lying tumbled on its side as if someone had thrown it down carelessly.

They all examined the box closely.

'This is the same one?' said the Fiddler.

'Oh yes,' said Sarah, 'though it looks a bit more battered than it did last time I saw it. What do you think Martin, was it like this this morning?'

Martin agreed with her. It was certainly the same box but a

splinter of wood had been knocked out of one corner, one of the little pillars in front of the doors had been cracked, and there was a mark on one side as if someone had kicked it violently.

'But where's Henry?' Lucy demanded anxiously.

'He may well be back at the farm having his tea,' said Sarah, making a great effort to sound sensible and cheerful. 'I think the first thing to do now is to go there and find out.'

But this took longer than they expected, for when they reached the road again they found that the tyres of Sarah's van had been slashed to pieces. The green car had gone, but Henry's jacket which Sarah had left in it, was lying in the middle of the road. This also was ripped apart.

'They've kidnapped Henry and done this to stop us chasing them,' Martin shouted angrily.

'They may have Henry, and then again they may not – even if we don't find him at home,' said the Fiddler. 'But whatever has happened, this is pure spite – the Lady would hardly need to use delaying tactics of this sort once she decided to make herself scarce.'

It was a long, hot walk back to the Partridges' farm, and Henry was not there when they arrived. Sarah told Mr and Mrs Partridge that they had found the Folly open and empty, and after waiting a little while, they had started for home. They had seen the old car, and recognizing Henry's jacket in it they had gone a little way into the woods to see if they could find him. On their return they found that someone had slashed the tyres of the van. She did not mention the box, because they had decided it would be best if that were to disappear for the time being. The Fiddler thought it would be safest with Lucy and Martin.

('There's one sound rule for dealing with magic,' he had said; 'when in doubt, leave it to a child.')

Mrs Partridge was extremely agitated, and immediately remembered the man in the bowler hat and his attempt to steal the box. She was not reassured by Martin unwisely mentioning the man's suspicious behaviour at the fair, but Mr Partridge told her not to get all worked up before she had anything to get worked up about. When he was driving them all home, however, he advised Sarah to tell the police about the damage to her van.

'And I think I'll just come along with you to the station and drop a word about this chap in the bowler that everyone keeps on about,' he added. 'No one's going to start worrying about a grown chap like Henry disappearing for an afternoon, but there's something funny about this box business.'

10

MORE ABOUT HENRY'S ADVENTURE

HENRY sat on the grass beside the box, his elbows resting on his knees, his head in his hands, trying to think very slowly and carefully over the last few minutes. At least, he had supposed it was only a few minutes that were involved, but of course it must be more than that, if the box had been removed and him with it between the time he entered it and the time he fell out of it. He must have fainted, he thought, probably when the box had lurched just after he had been shut in. He remembered that quite clearly – but then, he had thought that he remembered everything clearly, although the plain fact was that he had been in the box long enough to be conveyed in it to some place which was unknown to him. He must therefore have been unconscious for most of the time. He felt momentarily pleased with himself for having come to at least one logical conclusion: there was something comforting about being able to draw logical conclusions from the situation. He tried another.

The woman could not have removed the box by herself. It must have taken three or four men to carry the thing, so that the business must have been arranged between several people, and since someone had eventually let him out of the box, at least one of them must still have been around nearby when he got out. However he had seen no one. What logical conclusions could be drawn from that, he asked himself bitterly. One is lured into a box, removed to a remote part of the Park (he supposed it *must* be part of the Park . . . he quelled the doubt instantly; of course it was), and then simply left there – why? As he asked himself this question, something came into his head about a spear and a cauldron, and for a moment he felt very muzzy and confused again. That was what he was here for, wasn't it? To find the Spear and the Cauldron for the Lady? The moment passed and Henry shook his head irritably. It must be some kind of joke, though he had to admit to missing the humour of it completely. However, everyone said what a peculiar film it was that these people were making, and perhaps this was the sort of thing that had them all simply falling about with uncontrollable mirth.

Henry stood up and looked round the clearing once more, hoping to see a flash of green skirt somewhere – surely she must have stayed nearby to see what effect her 'joke' would have? He felt less than friendly towards his fascinating visitor, and he had two good reasons for wanting to find her: first he wanted to know where he was and what was his quickest way home, secondly he was warming rapidly to the idea of giving her a strongly worded piece of his mind about silly practical jokes. But there was no sign of the woman or her accomplices. He would have to find the way by himself.

As he tried to work out which would be the best direction to take, he was visited again by the uneasy thought that he might not even be in the Park now – he had not realized that it was so extensive, he certainly had not recognized that view of the Downs. But if this was not the Park, then he might have been unconscious for hours. He looked at his watch, shook it, held it to his ear and then stared at it in disbelief. According to his watch, which appeared to be running quite normally, he had been in the box no time at all. Henry was near to panic: could it be that this was not even the same day? His fears had hardly stirred, however, before they were allayed. He caught sight of a movement among the trees and a figure stepped into the clearing – a figure which under the circumstances comforted him mightily, although at another time it might have convinced him that his worst fears about his sanity were justified.

It was a bearded dwarf, brilliantly dressed in scarlet tunic, hose and hooded cloak, all of which burned with gold embroidery. He stood staring at Henry, thumbs hooked into his belt, while Henry stared at him. Obviously another member of the film company, Henry thought.

'Hel-*lo*,' said Henry, 'are you one of the jokers I have to thank for my little trip, or did you just happen to be passing?'

The dwarf continued to stare at Henry.

'Who are you?' he said flatly.

'I'm the twit who's just been carted here in that confounded box,' said Henry warmly.

Something that might have been a puzzled look stirred the dwarf's impassive features momentarily.

'How did you get here?' he asked in the same expressionless voice as before.

'I've just told you, haven't I?' said Henry shortly. 'Someone brought me here in that thing.' He jerked his thumb at the box.

The dwarf's eyes slipped briefly from Henry to the box and back again as if he had never looked away for a moment.

'Why are you here?' he demanded.

Henry was beginning to wonder whether this character really understood what he was saying. Perhaps he was a foreigner. He spoke in the over-precise way of someone who has learned a language perfectly but does not speak it often.

'Search me,' he began, then paused, for the dwarf had seemed to look puzzled again.

'I don't know,' Henry said more slowly and carefully, 'your leading lady, or whoever she is, wanted me to find some things for her, or at least that's what . . .'

He swayed slightly on his feet. Find some things, that was what he had to do. Some things the Lady wanted.

'Lady?' The dwarf had taken a few steps towards him, and there was a suggestion of urgency in his voice. 'Who is this Lady? What does she want?'

'A cauldron,' said Henry putting his hands to his face. His head felt as if it were going to burst and the air around him seemed to be humming. 'A cauldron and a spear.'

He felt a touch on his arm, and found that the dwarf had come up to him and was steadying him. He met the dwarf's eyes, strange golden eyes, and at once his head cleared again.

'It was a woman in green,' he said. 'She said she wanted me to help her find these props of hers. Then when I got into the box I must have blacked out or something, and somebody brought me here – in the box.'

The dwarf turned to the box and studied it for a few moments. He glanced briefly at Henry again, took a pace backwards, and then before Henry could begin to guess what he intended to do, ran at the box and kicked it mightily. Kicked it right off the ground in fact, right up into the air and over the tree tops. When he turned back to Henry the disturbance of his normally expressionless features was recognizable as a smile. He walked up to Henry and took hold of him by the elbows, as if he were about to swing a child into the air (though Henry was not less than eighteen inches taller than him). Henry had no time to realize what was happening, before he found himself being lifted off the ground. He seemed to be flying up to the tree tops after the box – or was it that he was falling? He was not sure really what was happening to him. . .

The sergeant at the police station took the damage to Sarah's van very seriously. He was also interested in the attempt to steal the conjuror's box, but as Mr Partridge had predicted he was not inclined to think that Henry's disappearance was anything to be concerned about. Lucy was rather shocked at this, but the sergeant said:

'If we turned out a search party every time some young feller wasn't where his friends thought he ought to be, we'd never have time for real criminals.'

To the children's surprise the Fiddler also went to the police station with them, giving the name William Schwartz and the Dublin address from which he had written to Sarah.

'Is it your *real* name then?' Lucy asked when they were all back in Sarah's sitting room. She sounded almost disappointed.

'One of my names,' said the Fiddler. 'A very respectable and useful one in fact. Mr Schwartz the violinist is quite well known and admired in certain circles, though after this it may be regrettably necessary to dispose of him. He has become a little too conspicuous lately. I shall miss him – and Dublin. I think he might disappear on a walking tour of the Dolomites. Mind you, the big consolation of this sort of life is that one repeatedly has the satisfaction of reading flattering obituaries of oneself.'

'Just don't try being too clever, that's all,' said Snowy darkly (he had been waiting under the arch when they returned). 'Or someone may have to write a real and final obituary for you.'

'That's precisely why Mr Schwartz will have to be suddenly taken from us when this business is over – because by that time I'm afraid too many people of undependable friendliness will have had the opportunity to put two and two together,' the Fiddler replied cheerfully.

'But we're going to get rid of the Green Lady, aren't we?' said Martin.

'I hope so,' said the Fiddler, 'but she isn't the only one who is ill-disposed to humankind – she just happens at the moment to be the most dangerous. There are plenty of others who will be very interested to know where I am and what cover I'm using.'

Lucy sighed.

'I thought everything was going to be all right, when she was gone,' she said.

'Everything can't be all right until *everybody* is all right,' Snowy snapped – he was still very irritable about the way the Lady's spell had whisked him back to the jug as soon as he came near her. 'As long as there are humans who are willing to be twisted, there'll be someone to twist them the wrong way. We may be able to get rid of the Lady, but the effects of her activities will still be with you, and there may be someone else who'll try to use the situation – that's something that your kind will have to deal with by itself.'

'Never mind what we're going to do when all this is over,' said Sarah impatiently. 'Let's think about what we're doing now. What about Henry, for instance?'

'That's all right,' said Martin. 'I'll go and find him.'

Everyone stared at him.

'You?' said Lucy. 'How?'

'Snowy said there was a way we could go across safely, so why shouldn't I go and find Henry now. He must be on the Other Side, mustn't he?'

'No good,' said Snowy.

'But you said – ' Martin was indignant.

'Things have changed in the last two or three hours,' said the cat. 'What's true in one situation isn't necessarily true in another. Think about it,' he leaned towards Martin and flicked his tail as he numbered his points, 'in the first place, if Henry is on the Other Side, at least one of the objects of sending you will have been achieved – he's bound to be picked up, and then it won't be long before someone will be trying to get in touch with us from there, which is what we want. Secondly, we have the box now, so that if he comes back through it he'll come here, so there's no need to worry about that, and if he's sent back some other way, he'll be sent by our friends by one of the Gates controlled from the Other Side, so there's no great chance of him falling into the Lady's hands when he arrives. Thirdly, there's no guarantee that we could send you to the same place over there as Henry has got to, and it would confuse things terribly to have tribes of people straying around with no idea of where they were or where they wanted to get to.

'I still think we should have acted sooner,' he concluded, 'but as things are, it's better to wait and see what happens next. We may not be able to do much at the moment, but if the Lady is relying on the box, neither can she.'

When Henry had not reappeared by the end of the week, the police sergeant visited Sarah, accompanied by another man in plain clothes. It was Friday afternoon and the children were with Sarah and the Fiddler in the sitting room after the shop had closed. They had just broken up for the Whitsun holiday but there was a noticeable lack of cheerfulness.

'I'm glad to find you all here,' said the sergeant. 'There were one or two more questions we wanted to ask you about young Mr Partridge and what happened the other day.'

He asked them to repeat their story and then he turned to Martin.

'When you were telling me about this on Sunday you said something about a smell in the Folly,' he said.

'That's right, and in the woods,' said Martin. 'Very sweet and horrible – sickly.'

'Ah,' said the Sergeant, 'it couldn't have been tobacco smoke could it? You wouldn't happen to know what cigarettes Mr Partridge smokes, would you? Or pipe tobacco?'

'It wasn't anything like cigarettes,' said Martin.

'And anyway Henry doesn't smoke at all,' said Lucy.

'He might when you're not around,' said the other man, 'so's not to give a bad example you know.'

'Oh no,' said Lucy confidently. 'I'd know because he'd smell smokey, wouldn't he? Like Daddy – he smokes a pipe – and Henry doesn't. Smell smokey I mean.'

The man laughed.

'Very sharp,' he said. 'We could train you as a police dog I reckon.' He turned to Sarah, who was looking very thoughtful. 'Do you know any friends Mr Partridge might have in London – anyone he might stay with for example?'

Sarah shook her head.

'No,' she said, 'and I think you're wrong.'

The man raised his eyebrows and the sergeant said:

'Wrong about what, Miss?'

'Well, it sounds to me as if you think Henry's mixed up in some drug thing, isn't that it?' said Sarah. 'And it's quite absurd.'

The sergeant looked very suspicious, but the man in plain clothes smiled.

'Dear me,' he said drily, 'how transparent we are Miss Peach. But are you quite sure you know Mr Partridge well enough to say that he could never be involved in anything shady?'

Before Sarah could answer the Fiddler joined in.

'*I* do not know the young man at all,' he said, 'but it occurs to me that the circumstances of his disappearance suggest that his "involvement" in whatever is going on – shady or not – was entirely involuntary. The object of interest appears to have been the box which his father mentioned – has that been found?'

'No, sir,' said the sergeant, glowering at him slightly, 'and that thought had occurred to us too, thank you all the same.'

The Fiddler bowed politely and the other man said:

'At the moment we are wondering whether something might have been hidden in that box, and possibly Mr Partridge interrupted a second attempt to steal it. Naturally, since the box belonged to him, we would like to know what, if anything, he had to do with whatever was afoot – if anything.' He smiled apologetically.

'Since we've nothing to work on except your description of a man in a bowler hat and a veteran car, which incidentally the Veteran Car Club knows nothing about, we have to grab at anything that might shed a bit of light on all this. I'd be very glad if you'd all think about what happened again, and let us know if you think of anything that might help – anything odd that's happened recently, even if it doesn't seem to have anything to do with this.'

Sarah said:

'We'll certainly do that, but I know that Henry had no idea of that box being anything special.'

'He was ever so surprised when the bowler hat man tried to take it,' Martin added. When the policemen had gone Lucy said:

'What's the use of telling them anything, if Henry's on the Other Side?'

'There's a lot of use in it,' said the Fiddler. 'Henry may be on the Other Side, but the Green Lady and her henchmen *must* be on This Side, and nothing would be more annoying or inconvenient to them than to be rounded up by the police for questioning. Remember that she has to work largely through human means as we do, and human means, however strange, could be quite extensively disorganized by a lot of suspicious policemen.' He grinned wickedly. 'It's up to us to give the police all the assistance we can.'

'Then it's a pity we don't know what really happened on Sunday,' said Martin. 'Like what she looks like now and who else was in it besides Bowler Hat.'

'That is the snag,' the Fiddler agreed.

The gloom occasioned by Henry's disappearance hung particularly heavy over the Lovell household that Whit week-end, because it had been suggested that it might be a good time for the children to be taken up in the balloon. On the Sunday morning Dr Lovell said:

'This is ridiculous. We can't all sit around for the whole holiday mourning the absence of Sarah's boyfriend. There'll be no ballooning now, even if he turns up today, so we might as well shove the tents into the car and go down to the sea for the rest of the weekend.'

It was a good idea, but it was defeated by circumstances. A thunderstorm hit the Lovell camp site on Sunday night, and on the way home on Monday they were stuck for hours in a traffic jam. Mrs Lovell and the children listened to Dr Lovell's poor opinion of the Machine Age and the corruption of Science for commercial ends, while they crawled home at less than a walking pace.

It was very late when they arrived back in Dunsley, so that it was not until the following morning that the children heard of Henry's return.

11

HENRY RETURNS

MRS LOVELL let the children sleep late the next morning and it was after eleven before they wandered into the kitchen in search of breakfast. Mrs Higgs was about to leave.

'What about young Henry then?' she demanded challengingly.

'*What* about Henry?' Martin replied, knowing that Mrs Higgs was not asking a question, but announcing her intention of telling them something.

'Kidnapped!' she whispered. 'Kidnapped by dope peddlers and dumped in Scotland – been unconscious for a week!'

'How do you know?' Lucy asked. 'They haven't found him have they?'

'Came back last night,' said Mrs Higgs, 'in a real bad state, so Billy Watt told our Ernie. All dazed and shaky. Billy said he couldn't think how he managed to find his way back from Scotland all by himself in that state. He met him in the lane, Billy did that is (he was up there to give Mr Partridge a hand), and he said he looked dreadful and didn't recognize him, Henry didn't—'

'Does Sarah know?' said Lucy.

'Went over to the hospital this morning,' said Mrs Higgs. 'Left the old gentleman in charge of the shop. He's a one, isn't he?' She went off into shrieks of laughter.

What the Fiddler had said to cause Mrs Higgs so much amusement remained unknown, because Martin and Lucy broke in together.

'The hospital?' Martin exclaimed, and Lucy said anxiously:

'What's wrong with him, Mrs Higgs?'

'Well, nothing much they think, but they wanted to be sure, that's all,' Mrs Higgs explained.

The children were in the shop waiting for her when Sarah returned in the early afternoon. Snowy slipped in behind her.

'How is he?' the Fiddler asked, looking up from a page of calculations with which he had been occupied.

'Pretty well considering,' said Sarah. 'Shaken, of course. From what he said I should think he did go to the Other Side.'

She flopped down in an ornate basket-work chair which everyone admired but no one wanted to buy.

'He's been allowed to go home now,' she went on, 'because they can't find anything physically wrong with him, but they filled him up with tranquillizers because he seemed very disturbed by it all.' She smiled faintly. 'He was quite sure he must be going mad, having hallucinations or something, the poor old thing. It all fitted with the drug idea of course, and that's apparently the line the police are working on.'

She told them the story Henry had told her, which was quite clear up to the point where he stepped into the box.

'He was very vague about everything after that,' she said. 'He said he thought that everything he could remember between then and when he came round to find himself wandering about in the middle of Glasgow must have been a dream.'

'And did he tell you anything about this dream?' said Snowy. 'It could be important.'

'He didn't want to talk about it,' Sarah told them, 'but eventually he said it was all like a very vivid nightmare, when you know you've got to do something, but don't know why. He said he thought he had to find a spear and a cauldron.'

Snowy hissed with excitement and the Fiddler said:

'The Tokens. Go on.'

'There wasn't much more to it. He said that this dwarf dressed up in red and gold came along and threw him up into the air, and he blacked out again. Of course it doesn't make a scrap of sense to him – does it to you?'

'Yes indeed,' said the Fiddler. 'Henry was really very fortunate – though I don't suppose he'd believe that – and so are we. The dwarf was the personal attendant of the Warden of the Marches, and now perhaps we can get on a little quicker.'

'How?' said Martin.

'If the Warden's dwarf met Henry and sent him back, he will certainly have alerted his master to look out for intruders on the frontier. That's one good thing. Another is that now I know where and when Henry returned to This Side, I shall be better able to work out where and when he got to on the Other Side. Then if you and Lucy will consent to take a message for me, I can hope to send you to the area where you are likely to meet the Warden or the Dwarf. It has to be you, I'm afraid, because it's safest for children and easiest – you are less tied to the time of this world anyway, you see.' He screwed up the paper on which he had been working. 'Was there anything else?'

'Only that the police are going to round up everyone who's had anything to do with the fair or the film in the last fortnight, so that Henry can see if he recognizes anyone,' said Sarah.

'Much good that'll do them,' Snowy sniffed.

'When can we go to the Other Side?' Martin demanded.

'As soon as I've worked out the best place for crossing from Jerome's tables,' the Fiddler told him, standing up and stretching. 'But as I'm no very brilliant mathematician that may take some time. I think I'd better start now.'

'It's a pity we can't get Daddy to do it,' said Lucy.

The Fiddler paused on his way to the door through to the sitting room.

'Of course, he's a mathematician, isn't he?' he said thoughtfully.

'I don't think he'd believe us if we—' Martin began.

'I'm sure he wouldn't,' said the Fiddler quickly. 'But I think I've heard his name mentioned in connection with something . . .

anyway it makes me think that his work might have some bearing on the matter, whether he would believe it or not. I hope the same thought doesn't occur to the Lady or any of her associates.'

'I'll arrange a guard,' said Snowy. 'She seems to have drawn off for the time being, but it's as well to be on the safe side.'

Snowy's precaution proved to be well-advised.

At breakfast the following morning Dr Lovell remarked morosely to his wife that there had seemed to be an extraordinary number of owls around the house during the night.

'Didn't you sleep well, darling?' said Mrs Lovell with mild sympathy. She always slept very well herself.

'Vilely,' her husband informed her. 'I don't know what the wretched birds could possibly have found to interest them in Akeman Street, but a pair of them was patrolling it all night. They were having a real party about three o'clock this morning from the sound of it.'

He turned to his post.

'Bills, bills, bills,' he muttered opening the first envelope. He stared at the contents in disbelief. 'Good Lord! This is ridiculous!' he exclaimed. 'I think today might as well be cancelled if it's all going to be like this!'

'What's the matter?' inquired Grandfather, who had just come into the kitchen.

His son held a piece of paper out at arms length and shook it.

'I have here a quarterly telephone bill that I doubt we could have run up in five years, apparently sent to me by some bungling computer,' he fumed. 'I wouldn't so much mind having my life run by machines if only they were efficient.'

'It's all your own doing,' said Grandfather. 'You scientists have mechanized the world for us – *and* provided the means to destroy the lot.' He turned to his daughter-in-law. 'Liz, have you still got my soft fruit book?'

'Father,' said Dr Lovell, screwing his face into an expression of anguish, 'computers and bombs are not by any means the whole of modern physics, whatever the newspapers might lead you to believe. Forget all that mad scientist stuff – electronic brains ruling the world and what not. As a piece of electronic engineering a computer may be marvellous – as a brain it's moronic.'

He stood up, tucked his newspaper under his arm and poured himself another cup of coffee.

'As it happens,' he continued, 'I have no more desire than the next man to have my life harried by a jumped-up adding machine or ended by an overblown firework.' He turned to the door. 'My son,' he said sombrely to Martin, 'if anyone ever tells you that you have a brain like a computer, which seems at the moment unlikely, take it as an insult. What they really mean, whether they realize it or not, is that you can't count past two, and spend more time messing things up than doing them properly. The real trouble with the confounded things is that people think they're so wonderful that they start getting as dim-witted as tin-can calculators themselves.'

He stalked off to his study with an air of saintly fortitude.

Within a few minutes he was back again.

'We had more than owls here last night,' he said grimly. 'It looks as if someone tried to break in by the study window. The window's broken, but they didn't actually get in, it seems.'

When the police arrived a short while later, they called at the shop as well, for Sarah too had been the object of unwelcome attention during the night, though there too nothing much had been done. The burglar had broken into the pottery, but something had apparently frightened him off. There were signs of a disturbance, a few pots had been knocked over and broken, but nothing had been taken.

Mrs Higgs was thrilled.

'I just had to come round and see that you was all right,' she said looking round eagerly, as if she expected to see a burglar hiding behind the door. 'You know what they was after, though, don't you?'

Mrs Lovell and the children shook their heads. It would not have surprised them at all if Mrs Higgs were to have told them that she had received a full account of the incident from a second cousin who knew the intruder personally.

'The Doctor's secrets!' she said triumphantly. 'It's obvious, isn't it? First they tried Miss Peach's and found they'd got the wrong house, then they come here. They was trying to get into his study, wasn't they? I bet he had a secret ray or something that kept them out!'

'I don't think Richard's doing anything very secret,' said Mrs Lovell, frowning slightly. 'He says he always tries to stick to things that have absolutely no practical application whatsoever.'

'Ah!' said Mrs Higgs, 'well he's clever, isn't he?'

Although they did not express themselves quite so melodramatically, the police seemed to have roughly the same idea. The sergeant was rather inclined to tie it up with the abduction of Henry and the other burglaries of a few weeks before, though more for the sake of having all the senseless crimes in one case than for any other reason, as he admitted to his colleague from the C.I.D.

'I sympathize,' said the other cheerfully, 'because if they aren't all in the same case, you've got the silliest crime wave here in Dunsley that I've ever heard of.'

Dr Lovell was incensed by the whole business. That anyone should have attempted to break into his home was bad enough, but that people should imagine him to be some kind of science-fiction character with secrets worth stealing was simply adding insult to injury.

The police were in the shop most of the morning, and as Wednesday was early closing day anyway, Sarah did not think it worth opening at all. Martin and Lucy went round as soon as the police left, but they had no time to discuss the affair before Henry arrived. He looked rather pale and very nervous, constantly jumping up from his chair and pacing round the room, or fidgeting with the money in his pockets. He evidently wished that the Fiddler and the children would go away, but since they showed no signs of obliging him, he eventually asked Sarah if she would care for a walk. Martin, thinking that a conference was needed immediately, would have tried somehow to dissuade Sarah and get rid of Henry, but the Fiddler urged her to go.

'You needn't worry about me or the shop, my dear,' he assured her in his godfathering tone, 'I'm quite able to amuse myself for an hour or so, and if the police come back I shall be here to attend to them.'

When Sarah and Henry had gone Martin said:

'Why did you do that? We need to talk.'

'What needs to be said now doesn't demand Sarah's presence,' said the Fiddler, 'and we don't want to antagonize Henry, do we? If we had to wait until he decided to leave, it might be midnight before we'd have a chance to get our heads together.'

They were in the kitchen, and the Fiddler started wandering around opening cupboards.

'You don't happen to know where Sarah keeps the salt do you?' he said.

Lucy showed him, and she and Martin watched with curiosity as he took the packet of salt outside and started to sprinkle it around, muttering to himself. He disappeared round the corner of the house, still sprinkling and muttering, reappearing a few minutes later, having apparently sprinkled salt all round the house. He stepped back into the kitchen, throwing down the last of the salt on the doorstep.

'Why did you do that?' said Lucy.

'Because I didn't at all care for the way my remarks about Dr Lovell's work were followed within hours by an attempt to burgle his study,' the Fiddler replied. 'I haven't the time, or indeed the special skills required to cast a magic circle, but that should be sufficient to keep anyone who's trying to spy on us at a distance for the moment. Many of the Old Ones, particularly those unfriendly to humankind, don't like salt or iron – ' he was now searching in Sarah's cutlery drawer, ' – so I think we can make ourselves fairly secure. We'll go into the shop and barricade ourselves in, as it were.'

He gave Martin and Lucy a handful of knives and forks apiece, and taking the rest himself he led the way into the shop. While they were arranging all the iron and steel objects they could find around the room, Martin suddenly thought of something.

'That must be why the Lady disappeared!' he exclaimed. Lucy and the Fiddler stared at him. 'They must have put Sir Archibald Thing's collection in a bank or somewhere like that during the war – and bank vaults are lined with steel, aren't they? So she'd be sort of screened, like radioactive stuff in lead.'

'My dear boy,' said the Fiddler with a gratifying hint of admiration in his voice, 'I should think you are very probably right. I wonder if that could suggest a way of securing her permanently. . .'

He drew the basket-work chair and two stools into the middle of the floor and they sat down. When the Fiddler put his hand into his pocket, Lucy thought he was going to play his violin again, but this time he produced a transistor radio.

'The marvels of technology are sometimes as useful to us as they are to her,' he remarked, tuning in to a programme of music and smiling with satisfaction. 'A Beethoven string quartet. It could hardly be better.'

'We're not going to sit here and listen to music are we?' said Martin in amazement.

'Martin, there are two things you should remember,' said the Fiddler. 'One, that music is a great power against evil and darkness; two, that good, loud music will cover anything we have to say should the eavesdropper be merely mortal.'

He turned up the volume and set the radio down on the floor beside them.

'Now, let's get down to business,' he said. 'You must have realized what was going on last night. Here I imagine they were looking for the box. At No. 28 I'm sure that it was a look at your father's papers they were after, with the idea that if they couldn't get the box, they might find something in his work that would help them to get through to the Other Side without it. They're not fools. Our great advantage is that they don't know about the Gates, but they could work it all out if they had a clue to it.'

'But Dad's work isn't magic,' Martin objected, 'it's science.'

'You could say exactly the same thing about the Gates,' said the Fiddler. 'It's all a matter of time and space and dimensions, which is what your father's work is about. I know that, because I've heard Jerome talking about him and what he's doing.'

'But why didn't they manage to break into our house properly,' Lucy asked, 'and why did they run away from here too.'

'That was the guard Snowy set. You may have heard them patrolling last night,' said the Fiddler. 'Not many people would stay around to be attacked by half a dozen owls. They must have dodged the guard here, but then there was another watchman inside. One that I didn't know about either, but Sarah showed me something this morning . . .'

He stood up and crossed to the big rocking horse.

'Look at this,' he said, tapping Horse's mouth.

The children joined him and looked. Caught between the clenched teeth was a shred of cloth, and there was a wicked look in the rolling eye. They remembered that last time they had seen Horse his mouth had been open.

The Fiddler returned to his chair and said:

'Sarah didn't have much time to tell me about Horse, but I think we can assume she's well protected.

'The next thing – the really important thing – is that I've worked out how I can send you across with least risk. I won't say any more about it now – ' his voice dropped to a whisper ' – I'll tell you what to do and what message you must pass on just before you go, but I want you to be here immediately after breakfast tomorrow morning. We ought to allow as much time as possible, in case I can't counteract the time distortion completely. I'll tell your mother that I'm going to take you out for the day – somewhere very educational, you know – I think St Albans would be suitable.'

He jumped up.

'Now we must tidy up – and not another word about anything – not even to each other – until we meet tomorrow morning.'

12

THROUGH THE EARTH GATE

THE next morning Martin and Lucy were ready early. The Fiddler had borrowed Sarah's van for the day, and they drove out of Dunsley as if they really were going to St Albans, but after a few miles the Fiddler turned off the main road, and returned, by many devious twists and back doubles, to the top of the Park Woods. At a point not far from where they had seen the green car, but higher up, the Fiddler pulled off the road and drove some way into the woods before stopping.

'We should be all right here,' he said getting out. 'I don't think we were followed, but just in case. . .'

He took a paper bag from his pocket and started sprinkling the contents round the van. The children thought it was salt again, but when he had finished the Fiddler set light to the white crystals. The fire licked quickly round the circle and then burned steadily with a pale mauve flame.

'If you want good old-fashioned magic,' he said, 'you go to a good old-fashioned witch, and fortunately I happen to know one.'

He dusted his fingers and took his violin from his pocket.

'I had an idea it might have been my old-fashioned witch who messed up the Lady's plans the other week-end, and I'm wondering now whether she can be prevailed upon to do something to keep Snowy off the jug, or I'm afraid we shall be deprived of his help as long as the Lady's at large in these parts. But old-fashioned witches aren't the most reliable of characters. They sometimes have schemes of their own. . .'

He started tuning his violin, talking all the time, not hurriedly, but as if there were no time to waste.

'I'm going to play you a lifeline, and as long as you hold on to it, you will still be in touch with your own time. You *must* hold on to it all the time. Keeping in touch with your own side may make everything on the Other Side look peculiar, but don't worry about that – I can't tell you how peculiar it may be, because I don't know.

'You should arrive very near the place where Henry went through, and as only a short time will have passed on the Other Side since he was there, the Dwarf, and perhaps his master too, should still be in the vicinity. I shall give Martin a whistle which will attract the attention of anyone within miles of the place. But when you come out on the Other Side you must just stand still and wait for someone to come – *you must not on any account go looking for someone*. Remember that the phases are against you and you must be very careful.

'When someone comes, you are to ask to see the Warden of the Marches. You must say that you have been sent by the Keeper of the Earth Gate – that and the whistle should be sufficient credentials – and when you meet the Warden you must answer any questions he asks you: call him "Your Highness" if you want to be really polite. You are to tell him all you know about the Green Lady and what she intends. Say that I think she must be isolated from both worlds and the box must be disposed of, but that to do both we need help from the Other Side – we need Jerome to help us to work it out, and we need power exerted from that side to actually do it. When you have finished and received his answer, turn round and follow the thread back. That's all there is to it.'

He handed Martin a small silver pipe like a penny whistle.

'Behind you is a path leading downhill into the woods. Turn round and walk down it when I start playing, and whatever you do *hold on to the tune*.'

Martin and Lucy turned to the path, and when the Fiddler started playing they set off hand in hand down the hill. The path

sank down between high banks which soon rose above their heads. The trees closed in, and presently they found that they were entering a tunnel. The sound of the violin grew fainter every moment, so that Lucy was afraid she must lose it altogether. Something tickled her ear. She put up her hand to brush whatever it was away and found herself holding a fine thread, which vibrated slightly. At the same moment Martin said tensely:

'I can't hear it any more.'

'It's all right,' said Lucy, showing him the silvery thread in her hand. 'I've got it here. If you put it to your ear you can hear the violin.'

They seemed to be walking a long time in the darkness: Lucy was comforted by the trembling thread in her hand; nevertheless she was beginning to feel uneasy as the tunnel went on and on. Just when she thought it would never end, they saw a glimmer of light ahead, and rounding a bend, they came out into sunlight again.

They were standing in a clearing in a wood so similar to the one they had just left that at first they wondered whether they had in fact crossed to the Other Side at all. However, they soon saw that everything looked slightly odd, as the Fiddler had said it might. It was difficult to say exactly what was wrong, but the scene did not look quite real. There was something insubstantial about it, and it looked, as the Fiddler had said when explaining the time distortion, like a picture turned slightly sideways. Martin wanted to go further, but as soon as they took a step away from the mouth of the tunnel, Lucy felt the thread tighten in her hand.

'We can't go anywhere. The tune won't come with us,' she said.

'Better see if we can get someone to come to us then,' said Martin putting the whistle to his lips.

He did not cover the holes or try to play it properly, but the little pipe produced a snatch of tune as soon as he blew into it. He stopped and stared at it in surprise.

'Go on,' whispered Lucy.

Martin blew into the pipe again and it played the same tune that the Fiddler had played for their 'lifeline'. When it came to the end of the tune, the whistle stopped playing, although Martin was still blowing into it. He lowered it from his lips. He and Lucy stared at each other and then looked round again.

'Doesn't seem to be anyone about,' Martin said. 'Do you think I ought to try again?'

Lucy gripped his arm and shook her head.

'Over there,' she said.

On the opposite side of the clearing stood a young man with white hair. He wore a short sleeved white tunic and a white cloak thrown back behind his shoulders. His legs and arms were bare, but he wore sandals that laced up above his ankles and leather braces on his forearms. He carried a bow, and a long knife hung in a sheath from his belt. Beside him stood the Dwarf. He walked towards them, the Dwarf following, and stopped in the middle of the clearing. Lucy tried to remember where she had seen such brilliant blue eyes before.

'We seem to be having a busy day,' he said. 'Who are *you* and what is your business?'

Martin said: 'We were sent by the Keeper of the Earth Gate and we have a message for the Warden of the Marches. Can we see him?'

The young man bowed slightly.

'If you have eyes,' he said.

'You . . . ?' said Martin doubtfully. He seemed to be finding difficulty in focussing properly on the young man and the Dwarf. Like everything else they looked thin and slanting.

'I am the Warden of the Marches,' said the young man coming up to them and holding out his hand. The nearer he came the more solid and real he became, until he looked quite normal. Lucy took his hand, which was reassuringly warm and firm, and curtsied neatly.

'Your Highness,' she said respectfully.

Martin managed some kind of bow and mumbled politely. The Warden smiled.

'I think we may dispense with ceremony,' he said, much to Martin's relief. 'Tell me your message.'

They told him the story of the Green Lady as far as they knew it, and explained about the box and the need to get rid of both that and the Lady. When they had finished he said:

'So that's it. The Lady thinks she can repossess the human world and she hopes to use the power of the Old Ones to do it, does she? I suppose the other one who was here just now was a servant of hers?'

The children looked at each other doubtfully, then Lucy said:

'Oh no, that was Henry. Did it seem like just now to you? It was more than a week ago to us. He's not really anything to do with her – he's one of us, though he doesn't know it – but perhaps she thought she could get at him because he likes machines and he's the Great Alectoris's grandson.'

The Warden seemed to have some difficulty in following this, and did not appear to find it very illuminating. He shook his head and said:

'He certainly wasn't very effective either as a spy or a burglar.'

He leaned on his bow for a moment frowning thoughtfully, and then he said:

'She is undoubtedly dangerous in your world, and we don't want her sending her minions here whenever she feels like it. The box is dangerous too. . . Yes, they must both be disposed of quickly, and the good mouse is just the person to devise the ways and means. But,' he straightened up, 'things are not quite as the Keeper of the Gate imagines, for she may send whom she will, they will not find the Tokens here.'

'You've hidden them already?' said Martin.

'I wish it were so,' said the Warden sombrely, 'but the truth is that she will not find them, because they are not here. They have been lost for many years now, and it is for that reason that our people have withdrawn from the borderland of our world and yours into their strong places, lest anyone should be planning to use our own power against us. That is why the Keeper of the Gate could not contact anyone, because only I and the Dwarf patrol the frontiers now, and it would be very difficult for anyone to attract our attention from your side, unless we happened to be in the right place exactly. It lightens my care to know that the Tokens have not been found in your world – I feared that more than anything – but things are bad enough all the same, and I can offer you less assistance than I might have in the old days.'

'How long ago did the Tokens disappear?' said Martin.

The Warden looked at the Dwarf who shook his head.

'It's difficult to say how long it would be on your side. . .'

'Before the old man came?' suggested the Dwarf.

The Warden snapped his fingers.

'Of course,' he said, 'it was not long before your great-great-grandfather, the sea captain came here. With all our people so anxious to leave the borders I was glad to have someone like him settled near one of the most frequented crossing points. The mice too are useful like that. . .'

'That was nearly a hundred years ago!' said Lucy.

'Was it?' said the Warden thoughtfully. 'And still they have not appeared in your world. Perhaps they are not there after all.'

'Why didn't you let the Fiddler or Snowy know about the Tokens?' Martin asked.

'It seemed better that as few people as possible should know,' the Warden explained. 'We did not want to advertise our weakness.'

'But they might have looked for them on our side for you,' said Martin.

'And others might have heard of their search, and might have tried some searching on their own behalf – others like the Lady. Now we can't conceal the matter any longer, but probably we should have had to ask our friends' help sooner or later anyway.'

The Warden thought deeply for a while.

'Here is what you shall say to the Keeper of the Earth Gate,' he said at last. 'Say: the Warden will send Jerome with all dispatch – but do not forget that in the present phase it may be weeks before he comes. You shall have all the assistance I can give, but it will be less than I could wish. Tell him about the Tokens, but in the name of every good thing be discreet about that, or there may come worse trouble than you have already.'

He fell silent again and the children thought he had finished. They were about to take their leave, when he said:

'Say this too: she that he knows of thrives still, and will come with me to the Well next time we meet there. That is all. He will understand.'

Martin and Lucy said goodbye then and had turned to go, in fact they were about to step back into the tunnel, when the Warden called to them. They turned back. He hesitated, and then said:

'The White Cat. . . ?'

Lucy said very quickly: 'He's fine. Everything will be all right when the Lady's gone.'

The Warden bowed and they entered the tunnel.

'Why did you say that?' Martin demanded. 'You don't know what's going to happen to Snowy when she's out of action again. It didn't get rid of the spell when she was shut up before.'

'I don't know,' said Lucy. 'I just had a feeling . . . he was terribly worried and I didn't want him to be . . . and anyway I should think Snowy would always be all right somehow.'

The tunnel seemed even longer on the way back, but at last Lucy felt the thread slip out of her hand and they heard the violin again.

The Fiddler had his back to the path, and did not turn round when they called. He did not look at them until they stood in front of him.

'Did you meet him?' he said.

They nodded and were about to tell him what happened but he shook his head.

'Not now, wait until we're in the car,' he said. His face was grey and weary.

The mauve flame still burned round the van. They climbed in and the Fiddler said:

'Now tell me.'

They told him all that had been said. When at length Lucy gave him the last message about meeting somebody at a well, the Fiddler bowed his head until his forehead rested on the steering wheel. Lucy touched his arm sympathetically.

'You must be tired. I suppose you don't do that often,' she said, thinking she understood why he had been so reluctant to send them across.

The Fiddler straightened up and smiled faintly at her.

'I am *very* tired,' he said, 'and I do *not* do that often. Very seldom in fact – and once I failed.' His knuckles whitened as he gripped the wheel.

Martin, looking at him curiously, noticed that his hands were not really old at all, and he realised for the first time that the Fiddler's present appearance was as much a disguise as the shape of the bronze statue had been. He must be much, much older than he looked, and yet Martin doubted whether he would look old if one could see him as he really was – except that one would probably not see him like that unless he was back on the Other Side.

'Why did *you* stay here?' he asked suddenly.

The Fiddler relaxed slowly and leaned back in his seat. He laughed softly.

'It was a spring morning when the choice came for me. I was sitting by the roadside on the way to Tara, playing at dice with Dearmid O'Dyna and losing every throw. If I lose again, I said to myself, I'm away out of here. I lost. I handed him the last bit of money I had on me and got up to be on my way . . . but there was a thrush singing in a hawthorn tree, and there was a girl in Leinster – and another across the water in Powys. . . It would take something stronger than ever I was to leave the spring of this world and two pretty girls into the bargain. . .

'But when ways part, in choosing one you must forgo the other. Those of us who stayed have never ceased to be useful and respected – most anyway – some have grown great again in different ways. But much has passed away from us that was beautiful, and they are hardly remembered now even in legend – the Shining Ones, the Danaans, the Old Gods.'

He fell silent again as if he had forgotten the children altogether and his eyes looked inward at his own thoughts. After a moment, however, he rubbed his face with both hands, stretched and fished a large pocket watch out of his inside pocket.

'Surprisingly enough it's only just lunchtime. I think we might substantiate our cover story by going on to St Albans after all,' he said.

13

JEROME

It was Sunday evening over a week later. Sarah and Henry were sitting at the table outside the pottery, playing chess. The Fiddler sat nearby on the bench, reading. Snowy was asleep beside him and Martin and Lucy were in the pottery up to their elbows in clay. For all of them it was the warm, peaceful conclusion to a long, hot, lazy day, and there was no sign of the weather breaking.

Henry was looking considerably less hollow-eyed and haunted than he had immediately after his disturbing adventure, though he was still jumpy and refused to talk about what had happened. At first he had felt vaguely ill all the time, and had been unable to sleep at nights, but that had stopped quite suddenly. Oddly enough it had stopped on the night he heard the owls hooting round the farm. At the time, lying awake and miserable in the hot darkness, he had thought savagely that a tribe of chatty owls was just about all he needed to ensure that he did not sleep a wink, but instead he had fallen asleep immediately. It had seemed all the more odd since his mother told him that the owls seemed to have decided to colonize the area, and had kept *her* awake every night for a week.

Martin and Lucy started to clear up the mess they had made in the pottery. They washed out the cloths they had been using to wipe down the table and wheel, and took them outside to dry. Snowy stretched and followed them down the garden to the clothes line. The Fiddler had said nothing more about his 'old-fashioned witch', but Snowy was almost always around now when they were all together.

Sarah looked up idly and watched the children and the cat,

while she waited for Henry to make his move. Something caught her eye – a bright speck in the sky.

'What's that?' she said pointing.

'Oh no,' said Henry, 'you can't distract me as easily as that. And anyway, I've got you. Checkmate Miss Peach!'

'Blow,' said Sarah looking at the board with mild surprise, 'I didn't see that.'

Henry laughed.

'You should have been watching the game instead of trying to cheat,' he said righteously.

'But there *is* something,' Sarah insisted. 'Look.'

Henry turned round and the Fiddler looked up too. The children ran back to them.

'What are you looking at?' Martin demanded.

'An aeroplane?' the Fiddler suggested.

'It doesn't seem to be moving fast enough,' said Sarah.

'Is it a satellite?' said Martin. 'Dad showed us one the other night.'

'I thought you could only see those in the dark,' Lucy objected.

'It's a meteorological balloon,' said Henry. 'I don't know quite what they do, but the weather station on the other side of the common from us puts them up, and they sometimes break loose.'

'Oh what a pity,' said Sarah. 'I was hoping for a flying saucer at the very least.'

Henry glanced at her and then looked at the speck again. He frowned.

'It's going to come across here,' said Martin. 'You can see it's coming nearer because it's getting bigger.'

'So it is,' said Sarah. Henry sighed with relief.

'Thank goodness for that,' he said.

'Why?' said Sarah, looking at him with surprise. He flushed with embarrassment.

'I thought I was seeing things again,' he said.

'Are you *sure* you were "seeing things" before?' said the Fiddler curiously.

'I was pretty sure a little while ago that I was going off my head,' said Henry shaking his head unhappily. 'It wasn't just the box business. There was the time when Martin was mucking about and I thought it really was that cat. . .' He glanced nervously at Snowy who had seated himself at his feet, grinning unnervingly.

The Fiddler raised his eyebrows.

'Given the choice between thinking myself mad and deciding that the world was not quite what I had believed it to be, I should choose the latter every time,' he remarked, 'but then I'm a few hundred years too old to have any very definite ideas about what the world really is like – that kind of certainty is the exclusive privilege of the young.' He grinned at Henry, who smiled uncertainly and said:

'Thank you, sir.'

The Fiddler bowed solemnly and returned to his book. Henry stood up.

'I ought to go now,' he said to Sarah.

'Shall I drive you home?' she asked.

'No, it's all right. I came down on my bike,' he replied.

They both went out through the gate that opened into the archway, and the others could hear them talking and laughing just outside.

'It's not a balloon,' said Martin suddenly in an odd, excited voice.

He and Lucy watched in silence as the shining object approached – swiftly now. The Fiddler closed his book, laid it on the bench and stood up. As it came in over the orchard of No. 28, they could see that it was not so large as they had thought. It was a disc, about six feet in diameter, with a transparent dome in the middle. Whisking low over the wall between the two gardens, it landed on the patch of grass, which in grandiose moments Sarah described as her lawn. The cockpit cover slid back and two very large black and white striped mice, each carrying an armful of notebooks and files, climbed out. They were nearly as big as Snowy, and Martin wondered if they could possibly have been as large as that in the days of their stage career. Snowy strolled up the garden path to greet them.'

'Is it Jerome?' Lucy whispered.

The outside gate banged and Sarah's footsteps could be heard echoing under the archway. Just inside her own garden gate she stopped.

'I should say Henry left not a moment too soon,' she said, closing the gate behind her.

'It would have been a most interesting situation,' murmured the Fiddler. 'But let me do the introductions.' He relieved the mice of their burdens and they climbed briskly onto the table. 'Lucy and Martin, allow me to present to you Jerome and Sylvester, once colleagues of Henry's late grandfather. Sarah of course needs no introduction, though I imagine she may have changed a little in ten or fifteen years.'

The mice bowed and shook hands all round.

'This is marvellous,' said Sarah, 'we didn't expect you for weeks.'

'So Snowy remarked,' said Jerome taking off his spectacles and polishing them vigorously with a large red handkerchief, which seemed to have come from nowhere. 'I must say I find it slightly puzzling, since I can't think of any reason why you should be expecting us at all.' He replaced his glasses and leaned forward beaming beadily at each of them in turn. Martin failed to see what happened to the handkerchief.

'You mean you haven't seen the Warden?' said Lucy.

'The Warden?' said Jerome. The two mice exchanged looks of surprise.

'Of the Marches,' Martin added. Jerome smiled at him.

'I rather thought that was who Lucy must mean,' he said. 'I was merely a little surprised. . .' He turned to the Fiddler and Snowy. 'Is one to infer that some action is imminent and our assistance required in that matter which we have discussed?'

'Look, hadn't we better go inside,' said Sarah, 'then we can explain everything.'

They settled down in Sarah's sitting room, the two mice and their masses of paper on a low table in the middle of the company, and the Fiddler explained what had happened so far. Sylvester nodded from time to time, and Jerome said: 'Yes. . . of course . . . quite so . . . I see,' whenever there was a pause.

'Now what about you?' said Snowy when the Fiddler had finished. 'How is it that you turn up so conveniently, just when you're wanted?'

'A most fortuitous circumstance,' said Jerome. 'We had no idea that things had arrived at this crucial stage. We were merely visiting Captain Lovell, and in the course of some purely mathematical speculations of interest to the three of us (and possibly to no one else), it occurred to us that it might be possible to apply our conclusions to the removal of both the Lady *and* the Conjuror's Box from *both* worlds – simultaneously. We had heard a whisper that things were moving again in this matter, and that Snowy was to be found here, and so we came along to offer our ideas.

'I suppose you'd agree that to dispose of both sources of trouble in a single operation would be the best we could do – but I don't suppose you've any idea of how it could be done, eh?'

The mouse beamed at them over the top of his spectacles. They all made polite noises of agreement.

'Of course not,' said Jerome, diving into a pile of notebooks and loose papers. After whisking about for a moment muttering to himself and making a kind of 'puttaputtaputta' noise, he found the file he wanted, opened it in front of him and removed a page covered with minute figures. He cleared his throat.

'We had several tentative plans. Which one we use must depend largely on the time and place most convenient for the operation. My own favourite idea is that we should entice the Lady into the box, and then project it into space at slightly better than the speed of light. She would be pushed out of time and space – through the grain of the universe, as it were, into – well – ' He dropped his paper and began to polish his glasses furiously.

'Outer space?' said Martin.

'Well no. More like *Other* Space – Somewhere Else – Absolutely Elsewhere,' said the mouse, disappearing the handkerchief and picking up the paper again. He tapped it with his glasses. 'I flatter myself that it's rather an elegant solution.' He coughed modestly.

'Don't you know where she'd be?' Martin persisted.

'Ah well, I have an *equation* you see,' said the mouse, 'but exactly what. . .'

Sylvester had sidled up to his brother and was looking over his shoulder at the page of calculations. He now whispered something in the other's ear. Jerome's beaming eagerness faded at once. His whiskers drooped dejectedly.

'Dear me!' he said. 'Do you really think so? Flashy? Dear me!'

He scuffled among the papers of the file, puttaputtaputting, while Sylvester whispered to him in a voice inaudible to the others.

'Look,' said Snowy with an exaggerated air of patience, 'I wouldn't want to seem boorish or stupid, but I imagine I'm speaking for everyone when I say that we are less interested in the grace and wit of your mathematics, than in the simple question: can it be done?'

Both the mice looked up with expressions of surprise.

'Oh no,' said Jerome, 'there isn't the power available. Even with the Tokens I doubt whether it could be done. In the present state of our knowledge – '

'Then why in the name of. . .' Snowy seemed to be as nearly speechless as it was possible for him to be.

'I just thought it was such a nice solution,' said Jerome looking very crestfallen.

'Have you any *possible* solutions – never mind whether they're nice or elegant or whatever?' Snowy demanded icily.

Sylvester nodded vigorously and Jerome brightened at once. His whiskers curled up springily once again.

'Oh yes,' he said, and went puttaputtaputta through the pile of notebooks.

'There is the cruder expedient of pushing her overboard, as it were,' he said, when he had found the one he wanted. 'You are all aware that the two worlds overlap in time and space (which is all one thing the way we're looking at it now), and that they are constantly in motion, which means that they are constantly joining and separating. What we must do is place the box in an area which is at present within the overlap, but where the worlds are about to draw apart. We get the Lady into the box, push the box halfway across the frontier, so that it is half in this world and half in the Other, and then as the worlds separate at that point, we push the box from both sides, and plop! out she goes through the gap!'

Jerome clapped his paws and looked around benignly.

'I'm sorry, but I'm afraid I still don't understand this about worlds overlapping,' said Lucy, 'and how can you push someone off the world?'

Jerome thought about it and then said:

'Overlapping isn't perhaps quite as accurate as we can be. You know that everything is made up of atoms?' the children nodded. 'And that even though everything looks very solid there's actually a lot of space between the atoms – even between the particles that make up the atoms?' They agreed again. 'Well, that's it, then. The two worlds aren't so much overlapping in fact, as sliding through each other – the atoms of one moving through the spaces between the atoms of the other. There's more than enough room, you know. It's possible to get from one world to the other by getting into one of the areas where both worlds are disposed in roughly the same manner – one does it by a system of coordinates which exist in both. It needn't worry you though – go on calling them Gates, just as everyone always has and you won't be a bit the worse off.'

'It's just a scientific description,' said the Fiddler reassuringly. 'After all, you don't find the floor any less solid because you know about the spaces between the atoms, do you?'

Martin looked uneasy.

'Why can we only see one world normally?' he said doubtfully.

'Because it's only if your atoms are lined up in the same plane as those of the Other Side that you can see it – your eyes belong in this world,' Jerome explained.

Snowy stretched and yawned prodigiously.

'I must say that it sounds nothing like my experience of either world,' he said, 'but then I don't pretend to be a scientist. However, if you clever chaps say it can be done, when can we get on and do it?'

Sylvester whispered urgently in Jerome's ear again, while Jerome took off his glasses and polished them slowly and reflectively this time.

'Ah yes,' he said when his brother had finished, 'there is one thing we ought to consider. *We* only know of two worlds crossing in this way – that is not to say, however, that there may not be many others. Now, if we push the Lady out of both our worlds, she won't be Anywhere to us, but that needn't mean she'll be Nowhere. We could be pushing our trouble into someone else's world. Sylvester thinks we should consider whether we have the right to do that, and I agree with him.'

There was a moment's silence in the room, and then Snowy sniffed and said:

'I think we must do what we can to remedy the trouble we know about, and leave the things we don't know about to look after themselves. There may not be any other places anyway.'

'I'm inclined to agree,' said the Fiddler slowly. 'Her power was surely born in the Other Side and operative in this – I should have thought it would have little effect on any third sphere.'

'It is a risk though,' said Sarah, 'and you did say she's not the only bad thing in our world – maybe when she's gone there'll be someone else just as bad, so we'll have endangered some other world without saving our own in the end. Isn't there any way of shutting her up here?'

'Of course, if she did get into another world, she might eventually exercise a *good* influence in it,' said the Fiddler. 'We mustn't forget she wasn't always bad even in this world – otherwise she would never have been entrusted with power. Her badness has been prompted by her desire for revenge on humankind – in another place she might come to her senses.'

'Then you want to proceed?' said Jerome. 'Very well, then it's just a matter of working out the best time and place, which Sylvester and I will set about at once.'

Sarah started to speak, and then hesitated. The Fiddler looked at her.

'You're worried about something?' he said.

'Well, it's just that I wondered what will happen to the Lady's spells when she's gone,' said Sarah. 'Will they just break, or what?'

'Precisely what I'm wondering myself,' said Snowy drily, 'but mine is a rather more personal interest, as you may imagine.'

'I wasn't thinking of you,' Sarah said.

'Dear Sarah!' said Snowy sweetly.

'It was Henry I was worried about actually. He's been different since he met the Lady, and it's not just shock or something sensible like that. He says he sometimes finds thoughts coming into his head that don't belong to him. He won't say much about it, because he thinks it sounds as if he's going crazy, but it's got something to do with the Tokens, and whenever it happens he feels ill. It makes me think she must have some power over him.'

The Fiddler looked very serious.

'This could be dangerous,' he said. 'You're right – she's obviously exercising some sort of influence over him. We must be careful when he is around. She may be using him to collect information. I'm sure he's not conscious of it—'

'Of course he isn't consciously working for her. And I don't suppose she's having much success getting anything out of him unconsciously either,' said Jerome indignantly. The others looked at him in surprise. 'Whatever made you think she could use him anyway?' he demanded.

'Well he *is* a bit machine-minded. And he doesn't believe in magic,' Martin said.

Jerome sniffed loudly and Sylvester shook with silent laughter.

'Not believe in magic? He's obsessed with it! Obsessed!' cried Jerome, whipping off his glasses and pointing them at Martin. 'Look at the machines he likes – straight out of a time when people *loved* their machinery and treated their engines like people. The Lady's idea is to have people treated like machines. Not the same thing at all, which is why she's had so little success with him.

'No, Henry's enthusiasm for engines is a disguised passion for *magic*. He's not a failed engineer – he's a frustrated magician. And if she had really taken him over, he wouldn't feel ill whenever she tried to use him, would he?'

They all agreed that Jerome was probably right.

There was a knock at the back door, and Sarah went to see who it was.

'That'll be Mum,' said Martin. 'We'll have to go now. Can you tell us when it's all going to happen?'

'Not yet,' said Jerome. 'We have to make a few important observations—'

'And in any case, it's better if you don't know anything,' Snowy broke in.

'We wouldn't tell anyone,' said Lucy feeling rather hurt that Snowy did not trust them.

'I'm sure you wouldn't,' said Snowy patiently, 'but you couldn't promise never to say anything about it to each other, and even that could be dangerous.'

'But you'll let us know what happens, won't you?' Lucy persisted.

'We can hardly avoid that,' said the Fiddler, 'seeing that you will have to be there. There's a part in this for everybody. You'll be told when the time comes.'

They could hear Mrs Lovell's voice in the kitchen, and then Sarah opened the door and told the children it was time to go home. Lucy followed her at once, but Martin hung back for a moment, remembering something he had wanted to ask.

'Jerome,' he said, 'if you could see *everything*, I mean *all* the worlds at once, what would it look like?'

Jerome closed his eyes and clasped his paws.

'I think,' he said, 'I *imagine* it might look something like – ' he took a deep breath, ' – an Infinite Shimmer.'

14

ST JOHN'S EVE

DURING the week that followed Martin and Lucy spent as much
time with Sarah as ever, but saw nothing of the mice, or Snowy,
or even the Fiddler. Mrs Higgs informed them at the beginning
of the next week that 'Mr Schwartz' had gone away, and was off
to some mountains in Italy, but when they tried to ask Sarah
about him, she changed the subject at once, and they understood
that there was a complete ban on conversation which had
anything to do with the Green Lady.

That Friday evening Dr and Mrs Lovell were going to the
theatre in London and intended to stay the night with Aunt Bea,
leaving Martin and Lucy in the care of Sarah and their grandfather. The arrangements were simple: Sarah would feed them,
and the door between Grandfather's flat and the upstairs of No.
28 would be left open all night. The children approved of this, and
assured their parents that they might stay away the whole week-
end, if they felt like it, for neither Sarah nor Grandfather had more
than the haziest idea of what their proper bedtime should be.
Mrs Lovell looked faintly suspicious, but went off telling herself
that *she* was going to enjoy herself, so perhaps it would be mean
to impose petty restrictions on her children.

Sarah was going out with Henry later, and so when they had
had dinner with her, the children spent the rest of the evening
with Grandfather. As Mrs Lovell had guessed they might, they
went to bed very late. Grandfather knew more stories than any
ordinary person they knew (it would not be fair to count people
like Snowy and the Fiddler), and he loved telling them, so that
it was only when he noticed that it was nearly dark and both the

children were beginning to yawn, that it occurred to him to send them to bed.

It was another hot night, but the air had been heavy all day and it felt as if the heat wave were brewing up a thunderstorm. Lucy fell asleep on top of her bed, with her window half open.

Some time later she woke suddenly and completely. She had no idea what time it was. The air was still stiflingly warm, and the panel of moonlight that lay across the room looked as if it had been cut out of the solid darkness with a knife. Lucy felt her ears stretch and twitch like a cat's, as she tried to hear again the sound that had woken her. In a moment it came again: a rustling and scratching from the window. A dark shape rose on the window sill against the moonlight – the shape of an extraordinarily large mouse.

'Jerome?' said Lucy sitting up.

'Ah,' said the mouse leaning forward, 'I thought I might be in the right place.'

'*I* thought you might be someone come to steal the box,' said Lucy, giggling with relief. She reached out to turn on her bedside light.

'Can you manage without the light?' said Jerome.

'What is it?' she asked, knowing already.

'Everything is set for tonight. St John's Eve – Midsummer – Beltane – you know. Very good time for things like this.'

It took Lucy no more than a few minutes to dress in jeans and a tee shirt.

'I should take something warm,' Jerome said as she turned to the door, 'it's not cold now but it could be later. And bring Snowy's jug. He won't be on it – he's gone ahead, but he thinks someone ought to take it because we don't know what will happen to her spells.'

Lucy took her anorak from the back of the door as she slipped out, and put the jug in her pocket.

The passage was dimly lit by a light shining through from

Grandfather's flat, but Lucy could hear no sounds of movement, and so she assumed that Grandfather must have gone to bed, leaving the light for them in case they wanted him in the night. When she opened Martin's door he was already sitting up in bed.

'You'd be a useless burglar,' he said, 'I heard you clogging along the passage right from your room.'

'I don't want to be a burglar, so it doesn't matter, does it?' said Lucy.

'What's up anyway?' her brother said.

Jerome jumped up on the bed.

'It's tonight,' he said.

While Martin dressed, Jerome told them the plan and what they were to do.

'Snowy has put about a rumour that the Fiddler has discovered a way of using the box to get to the Other Side himself, and that he intends to get the Tokens for his own use. She knows now that the Fiddler is one of the Old Ones, so she thinks that if he has found a way of beating the ban, it will work for her too. We shall take the box to the place we have chosen, and arrange everything as though the Fiddler were going to enter the box at the appointed time, but we expect her to intervene and get into the box herself. Then we must all heave-ho for all we're worth. We have had a message that the Warden and all the forces he can muster are waiting along the present frontier, and Sylvester has taken our vehicle back to fetch Captain Lovell, who will be able to help us best over Here – being human, you see.'

'Where is the place?' Martin asked, pulling on his anorak.

'The roof of Waddesworth Manor, and the time will be just before dawn,' Jerome said. The children stared at him in amazement.

'How on earth are we going to get there?' said Martin.

'Lucy will go with Sarah, you'll see how in a minute,' said Jerome calmly. 'Martin must ride up to the farm and persuade Henry to get out his balloon—'

'Henry won't do that in the middle of the night,' Martin exclaimed, 'he'll think I'm having him on.'

'You will say that Sarah needs his help, that should encourage him,' Jerome said, 'and I will go with you. He should recognise me from what he knows about his grandfather's act. Have you a basket or saddlebag I could ride in?'

Martin had not, but Lucy suggested that he might carry Jerome in his duffel bag, and they crept cautiously downstairs. Jerome stopped at the back door.

'Better give the box to Lucy,' he said. 'She and Sarah will get there before us.'

'But what are we going to do?' Martin asked as he let them out quietly.

'What you did when you drove the Lady away from the box in the woods,' said Jerome. 'Push her away with your thoughts. There will be others to help.'

'How can Henry do anything?' Lucy asked. 'He won't even believe in it.'

'Henry will be anxious about Sarah, and if he recognizes the Lady, he'll be very resentful about the way she treated him before. Chivalrous and indignant – that could be very effective. Anyway, we may need his balloon to get away. The whole area could be quite dangerous for a while.'

Jerome sent Martin to fetch his bicycle and led Lucy under the archway, where Sarah was waiting. Lucy immediately understood how she and Sarah would travel to Waddesworth, for there stood Horse, looking taller and stronger than ever. He shifted his feet and shook his head impatiently, so that his elaborate harness chimed softly and glinted in the darkness. Sarah patted his shining blue neck and led him out onto the Lovells' lawn. Jerome disappeared after Martin.

'There's more room to take off here than in my garden,' she whispered to Lucy. 'Can you get up?'

Horse was very large for a rocking horse, but in the scale of natural horses he was no more than a small pony. Sarah held the box and Lucy mounted without any difficulty, except that she was clumsy with nervousness.

'Sit well forward,' Sarah said. 'Sit on the pad at the front of the saddle, so that I can get up behind you.'

She handed the box back to Lucy and mounted behind her. Like the children she was wearing jeans and anorak, but she shivered slightly, and Lucy knew that she too was nervous and excited.

Martin appeared from the direction of the old stable, wheeling his bicycle, his duffel bag with Jerome's head poking out of the top, slung across his back.

'Good luck!' Sarah called softly.

'We shall need it, if we're going to get Henry out,' Martin said. 'Good luck.'

'Away we go then,' said Sarah.

Horse tossed his head and cantered across the lawn. Two, three strides, and then his hooves were no longer thudding on the grass. He seemed to be moving like a horse galloping in slow motion rising over the orchard wall at the end of the garden and wheeling back over the house in a wide sweep. Sarah held Lucy firmly, and Lucy clung to the box.

'Do you know the way?' she asked anxiously.

'No,' said Sarah, 'but the owls do.'

She pointed towards the trees in the garden below. Four tawny owls and three barn owls slipped out of the shadowy branches, rose to them on great silent wings like enormous moths, and grouped themselves round Horse with one of the barn owls in front to lead the way.

'They are a guard too, in case anything tries to stop us,' Sarah explained.

Although his movements were slow and dreamlike, Horse passed swiftly southwards over the sleeping countryside. The moon was low in the sky now and the stars looked very small and distant in the high roof of the night, when Lucy looked up. The air was warm and soft, the sky clear, except low in the west where clouds were gathering in a spreading haze. Lucy's nervousness passed and she leaned back against Sarah's shoulder, feeling peculiarly calm and unreal, as they rode through the short midsummer night.

While Sarah and Lucy swept across the night sky, Martin toiled gloomily up the hills on his bicycle in roughly the same direction. He had no hopes whatsoever of persuading Henry to take him seriously.

When he arrived at the farm, he propped his bicycle by the back door and threw a handful of earth at Henry's bedroom window. There was no response and so he tried again. He was about to look for a few small stones, when the window flew open and Henry's head appeared.

'What the blazes is going on?' he demanded irately. 'Who's there?'

'It's me – Martin. Sarah needs you,' Martin called warily.

'Hell's teeth!' said Henry forcefully. His head disappeared. In a matter of minutes the back door opened and Henry, in slacks, sweater and sandals came out.

'What's the matter with Sarah?' he demanded sharply. 'Where is she?'

'On the roof of Waddesworth Manor. We've got to go there in the balloon. . .'

Henry folded his arms and leaned against the wall.

'I see,' he said slowly. 'You want me to get out the balloon and take you to Waddesworth Manor in the middle of the night. You want me to believe that Sarah is already there – on the roof. I see.' His eyes narrowed.

'I won't waste my time asking you how she is supposed to have got there or why,' he went on, 'but I *would* like to know how you have the almighty nerve to come and wake me up at this hour with a yarn like that. I suppose it's another of your peculiar jokes,' he concluded bitterly.

'It's no joke, Henry,' said Jerome, popping his head over Martin's shoulder. 'Let me out of this bag, Martin, and I'll try to explain.'

'You're telling me it's no. . .' Henry began, and then stared goggle-eyed while Martin released Jerome from the duffel bag. Talking cats had no particular significance for Henry, and he could manage to ignore one when he met it, but large black and white striped mice had been part of his childhood dreams. To deny a striped mouse when it addressed him, would have meant denying far too much that was essential in his imaginative make-up.

'Good!' said Jerome shaking himself. 'Good evening, Henry (or rather I suppose it should be good morning now). You won't know me, but I expect you know *of* me – I was one of your grandfather's mice. Not quite so big in those days, but that's something I'll explain when we have more time – in the balloon.'

'No, you couldn't have been so big. . .' Henry's voice trailed away and he bent down to look at Jerome, who held out his right paw politely.

'I'm dreaming,' said Henry.

'It doesn't really matter much whether you are or not,' said Jerome reasonably, 'it certainly has no bearing on whether or not you get your balloon out.'

'No?' said Henry. 'But surely I'm not going to get the balloon out just for a dream, am I?'

'Dear me, dear me,' said Jerome, 'you must try to be consistent. If you are dreaming, then you will be dreaming that you're getting the balloon out as well, won't you? Either it's all a dream, or it's all real. If it's a dream, you might as well go along with it and see what happens. If it's real – well, here you are being lectured by an unnaturally large, striped mouse. *That* should indicate that something peculiar is afoot. Quite as peculiar, for

instance, as Sarah being on the roof of Waddesworth Manor.'
He beamed at Henry and polished his glasses with a flourish.

'But I can't take the balloon up at night – and it doesn't steer
very well anyway,' Henry objected dazedly.

'We can attend to that in no time at all, dear boy – I promise
you,' said Jerome, settling his spectacles back on his nose again.
(Martin still did not see what happened to the handkerchief.)
'Just lead the way.'

15

THE BATTLE OF
WADDESWORTH MANOR

THE owls brought Sarah and Lucy the last mile or two of their way by a low concealed route through the woods which encircled the Manor on three sides. The moon had set now, the clouds from the west covered half the sky and the strip of park between the woods and the house was pitch dark. Horse and the owls skimmed across it like the shadow of a cloud, and landed among a cluster of chimneys at one end of a flat roof. Sarah slid off the magic horse's back; his head was drooping now and he was plainly tired. She helped Lucy to dismount and then found some sugar lumps in her pocket for Horse.

'Poor old lad hasn't been out for ages,' she whispered.

'Will he be all right by the time we go back?' Lucy asked.

Sarah shrugged and said:

'I don't know. I hope so.'

'I too,' murmured the Fiddler, suddenly materializing in the black shadow beside them. 'We may need to leave in a hurry, and I should like to know that you can get away even if Henry doesn't arrive in time.'

'Where is he?' said Snowy, slipping between them and looking through the ornamental battlements which surrounded the roof. He turned back to them. 'He ought to be here by now.'

'He can't go faster than the wind,' said the Fiddler, 'and it's better that he should not arrive too soon. A balloon is a tricky thing to hide, don't you think?' Snowy muttered something and sat down beside them, his tail twitching nervously.

'How long?' whispered Sarah.

'Soon,' said the Fiddler. 'Have you got the box?'

Lucy handed it to him. She was shivering again with excitement, and the Fiddler tucked the box under one arm and put the other reassuringly round her shoulders.

'Just time for a last word about what's going to happen,' he said softly. 'In a minute I shall go and place the box on that skylight in the middle of the roof. I shall stand back until it has grown full-size, and then it will be time. I shall start to play and walk towards the box – I expect to be stopped before I reach it. Once she is inside you must *push* with your thoughts, with all your strength. Don't take any notice of anyone else. There will be others around by then, but they will only be here in their dreams.'

'Are you going to wait for Henry?' said Sarah.

'We can't wait for anything now,' the Fiddler told her firmly.

They stood in silence among the chimney stacks, looking out across the expanse of roof to the skylight which stood like a platform in the middle. The warm heavy air stirred a little, and the Fiddler turned his head to the slight breath of wind.

'Henry will be here soon,' he murmured. 'Let's hope he beats the storm.'

'What about Captain Lovell?' said Lucy.

'I doubt whether he'll make it now,' he hugged her lightly. 'Ready?'

Sarah drew in her breath and took Lucy's hand as the Fiddler stepped away from them. He looked back and smiled, and then hurried to the middle of the roof, where he set the box down carefully on the skylight. When he backed away from it again, Sarah and Lucy could hardly see him in the darkness. Snowy edged in front of them and stood watching intently. There was a distant rumble of thunder behind them, and another stronger gust of wind lightly buffetted their backs.

Suddenly the darkness in front of them seemed to lift a little, and they could see the box standing man-sized on the skylight. At the same moment they heard the violin playing softly and jauntily, and saw the Fiddler stepping slowly towards the box. The doors opened. It was still very dark, although it seemed to be much lighter in the vicinity of the box. As the doors opened, the darkness was suddenly full of moving shapes which converged on the Fiddler. He disappeared among them, the violin stopped abruptly, and a tall, green cloaked figure stepped into the box. The doors closed and the Lady's followers gathered round the box to prevent anyone else approaching it. Away on the far side of the roof the violin struck up again, wildly, mockingly now, and Snowy shouted:

'Now! Push!'

The darkness rustled around them as Sarah and Lucy braced their minds to thrust the Green Lady out of their world, as though an invisible company were bending to the same task. The box seemed to flatten and turn sideways.

'Push!' cried Snowy again.

The box stopped and strained back a fraction. The Lady had realized that something was wrong and was trying to return. One of the doors sprang open.

'Pu—'

The white cat's voice broke off suddenly as a wave of icy air and a sickening smell broke over them from the direction of the box. Fearfully Lucy put her hand in her pocket, to feel the china cat hard and cold on the side of the little green jug. The box turned back further and began to look more solid again. The invisible throng faltered.

Lucy and Sarah willed the box to turn with all their strength, but still it came slowly back. The light round it was growing, and they could see the Lady standing at the open door. The situation was deadlocked: the Green Lady could not leave the box, and her enemies could not push the box out of their world. Her followers milled around the skylight now, not knowing what to do. The box shuddered and Lucy and Sarah felt the Lady's cold malevolence sweep across them again. Sarah pulled Lucy behind one of the chimney stacks.

'Keep out of her line of fire,' she said. 'Remember Snowy.'

Lucy gripped the china cat in her pocket and tried to fight down her fear. A huge shadow loomed behind them. They swung round to meet some new menace and saw the blue and silver sphere of Henry's balloon dropping out of the heavy clouds which had come up with it. When the basket was level with the battlements Martin and Jerome climbed out, Henry secured the balloon to the battlements and followed them, looking round anxiously.

'Here!' Sarah whispered urgently.

Henry, Martin and the mouse joined them behind the chimney, and Sarah explained what was happening as well as she could in a few seconds. Henry looked across the roof at the box, which was rocking now in the grip of the contrary forces being exerted on it.

'We've got to shut that door,' he said, 'and spin her round into the middle of the box.'

He slipped out from the shelter of the chimney stack, but Martin was ahead of him.

'It's safer for children,' he whispered as he darted away.

He dodged round the crowd of the Lady's followers, who were still trying to find the Fiddler in the darkness to silence his powerful music. Henry swore and ran after him. Lucy and Sarah saw Martin reach the skylight, and Henry had almost caught up with him, when he stumbled and several of the Lady's people jumped on him.

Martin ignored the scuffle behind him and jumped on to the skylight beside the box. The Lady did not see him until he took hold of the door to slam it shut on her, then she turned and looked at him and for a fraction of a second Martin felt the petrifying fear of her fury. But the door was already swinging shut, and the boy was shielded from her power before it could bite. He was still standing dazed and breathless on the skylight when Henry jumped up beside him, thumped the side of the box low down and towards the back, and then pulled Martin away.

'Not a healthy spot,' he panted, making for the edge of the roof.

As soon as Sarah saw Henry and Martin dive away from the box, she shouted:

'Now!'

The indistinct army of shadows around them gathered its strength and swung forward. Sarah and Lucy could almost see them now on the edge of their vision.

'Again!' shouted Sarah. 'Push – her – OUT!'

The darkness heaved. The box swung slowly like a door on stiff hinges, until it looked no thicker than a post. The violin came fiercely towards them, rising at last to a savage crescendo, and falling suddenly silent. A distant horn sounded in the silence. Another rumble of thunder. Lucy and Sarah saw the roof in front of them shiver. The horn sounded again, nearer, and everything began to shake gently. The Lady's people were in confusion now. One or two ran up to the box and were immediately whipped round like dead leaves in a wind and disappeared. The others ran to the edges of the roof. The light round the box was growing and shimmering like a heat haze. The third time the horn was blown it sounded only yards away.

'Push!' Sarah whispered hoarsely, and the box seemed to shrivel in a blaze of white light.

Sarah clung to Horse's neck and leaned on him for support. Lucy sat down by one of the chimneys clutching the tiny Snowy in her pocket and crying, more from weariness than anything else just then. She heard the Fiddler's voice close by:

'Come away from here, it's not safe. Where's Lucy?'

'Here,' she said stumbling to her feet again.

The Fiddler picked her up and carried her to the edge of the roof. Sarah followed leading Horse.

Henry and Martin emerged from the darkness to meet them.

'We should get off as quickly as possible,' said the Fiddler. 'We must have been stronger than we thought: we've created a maelstrom here, and if we stay much longer we shall be sucked into it too. How's Horse?'

'Very frightened and tired,' Sarah said doubtfully. 'I don't know if he'll be able to take us—'

Lucy said:

'If Sarah goes in the balloon with Henry, perhaps Horse could manage Martin and me.'

'Good,' said the Fiddler. 'In you get, Sarah. Henry, I'd advise you to get clear of the woods and then land. You don't want to get caught up in this storm.'

Sarah seemed inclined to argue, but Henry bundled her into the basket and cast off immediately. The balloon lifted away from the Manor once more and drifted across the park glimmering magically. There was a flicker of lightning and the thunder rolled nearer.

The Fiddler put Lucy and Martin on the rocking horse's back, but he was still unable to take off.

In the east the sky was beginning to lighten, but the storm was rolling up swiftly to swallow the dawn. A long gust of wind swept the roof of Waddesworth Manor and the rain began to fall. The Fiddler turned to look at the place where the box had stood. The children turned too. There was nothing there now but a trembling haze. The whole roof was apparently becoming transparent and other shapes were showing through. The thinness was flowing slowly but steadily towards them.

'It's a useless thing to say I know, but I'm most terribly sorry about this,' said the Fiddler quietly. 'It looks as if I've bungled it in the end. I've no idea what's going to happen now, or where we shall find ourselves, but I hope we shall be *somewhere* and together. . .'

'There's no need for anyone to go anywhere alone or in

company, as far as I can see,' said a voice from the edge of the roof. They turned back to see Jerome, whom they had all forgotten, sitting on the battlements and pointing upwards.

'Less heroic to be rescued, but preferable I think,' he added drily.

A dark mass was descending to the battlements. At first they thought the balloon had returned somehow, but as it settled alongside the roof, they saw that it was in fact a small sailing ship. An old gentleman with white hair and glasses leaned over the side.

'Is it Captain Lovell?' said Lucy.

'Who else?' said Jerome, polishing his spectacles happily.

Lucy and Martin slipped from Horse's back.

'Ahoy there Waddesworth Manor!' called the Captain cheerfully, pushing a gang-plank across to the battlements. 'What's to do?'

Jerome ran across followed by the children leading Horse, and lastly the Fiddler.

'Morning, Captain,' said the Fiddler. 'I think we'd better be away sharpish, if that's all right with you.'

As the ship rose away from the Manor, a terrific flash of lightning ripped the sky open and for a split second illuminated two overlapping landscapes – Waddesworth Manor and behind it a range of low hills, like two backdrops painted on gauze. Behind both a third was dimly visible, and vast, vague shapes seemed to be striding through them all. The thunder crashed almost overhead and everything disappeared in a curtain of rain.

'Better get under cover,' said the Captain.

It was a very small ship, with only one mast and a little wheelhouse amidships where Sylvester was poring over a chart. As they were all crowding in, the ship rolled unexpectedly and Lucy stumbled. The hand holding Snowy flew out of her pocket as she fell. The jug slipped through her fingers and smashed against an iron ring on the deck.

16

THE END – IN A
MANNER OF SPEAKING

HALF blinded by tears and rain Lucy fumbled on the deck for the fragments of china. She stood outside the wheelhouse holding the broken pieces, unable to go in and face the others. She had broken the jug. She had killed Snowy just when his enemy was beaten.

The Captain came out again.

'Hey! What's this?' he said. 'What's the matter with our little gel?'

Lucy showed him the broken china.

'What's this then?' the Captain asked peering at the pieces. 'Come inside and let me find me other spectacles.'

'I've killed Snowy,' Lucy gasped.

The Captain stared at her, glanced back into the wheelhouse and then laughed. Lucy looked at him in horror.

'Well, if you've killed Snowy, I reckon he makes a rare lively corpse,' said her great-great-grandfather, patting her shoulder. 'Come inside and join the wake.'

He pushed her gently into the little cabin where Snowy was sitting with Martin and the Fiddler on a bench that ran along one side. The two mice sat on a table at the other side, busily working out their course.

'You are a twit Lu,' said Martin. 'Snowy's in here.'

'I thought he was on the jug when I dropped it,' Lucy said, rubbing the tears away from her eyes.

'I was,' said the white cat, calmly washing his face.

'Then—'

The Fiddler interrupted her.

'You broke the spell when you broke the jug,' he told her. 'This ungrateful brute should be humbly thanking you, instead of allowing you to be abused.'

Snowy jumped down and rubbed himself round Lucy's ankles. When she reached down shyly to stroke him he looked up at her, his blue eyes twinkling and his curly smile creeping into the corners of his mouth. He purred softly and Lucy burst into tears again. The white cat jumped back onto the bench grinning.

'Now what is it?' he demanded. 'It's wet enough outside without bringing the rain in here too. Come and sit down and stop blubbing.'

'But why did the Green Lady do that?' Martin said. 'It seems silly – I mean, the jug could have been broken accidentally any time.'

'It could,' the Fiddler agreed, 'but on the other hand Snowy and everyone else thought as Lucy did, that if the jug were broken Snowy would be killed, so he and all his friends would take particular care to see that it didn't happen. That's to say all the people most anxious to unspell Snowy would be taking most care not to do the one thing that would release him. Not quite so silly, you see. . .'

The balloon drifted low over Waddesworth Woods, and then Henry started to let the gas out slowly and dropped the trail rope.

'If we get caught up in that storm we might be blown miles high,' he said.

They landed in a field just as the first of the rain caught up with them. They stowed the balloon in the basket as well as they could, hauled it under the shelter of a hedge, and set off for the main road hoping for a lift.

By the time they were picked up a few miles from Aylesbury by a lorry they were soaked to the skin.

'Breakdown?' the lorry-driver inquired sympathetically.

'I'll say so,' said Henry, giving Sarah a helping shove up into the cab. 'It's the last time *I* try to save time and miss the traffic by driving through the night. . .'

Captain Lovell brought his ship in over the orchard of No. 28

and moored her to an apple tree. When the children started to say good-bye to him he said:

'Not just yet, I'm coming down to the house with you. It's the dickens of a long time in anyone's world since I saw that young grandson of mine, and now I'm here I can't go off without dropping in for a word. Jerome and Sylvester can take the ship home for me.'

'How will you get home?' Lucy asked.

'Snowy's going to fix that, aren't you matey?' said the Captain, rubbing the white cat's ears with a familiarity he would never have permitted to anyone else.

Captain Lovell dropped a rope ladder over the side and they all climbed down. Horse now managed to take off from the deck and flew over into Sarah's garden.

At the back door of No. 28 the children said good-bye to the Captain, the Fiddler and Snowy in the grey dripping dawn.

'Shall we ever see you again?' said Lucy a little shakily.

'Maybe,' said Snowy, 'and then again, maybe not.'

'You might not recognize us if you do,' the Fiddler warned them.

But Captain Lovell said:

'I reckon you will – sometime.'

Martin and Lucy stood at the door and the Fiddler waved good-bye to them as he disappeared round the corner of the house. They heard him whistling jauntily under the archway. The outside gate banged and he was gone. Captain Lovell shooed them inside the house, and he and Snowy turned to Grandfather's front door just by the arch. . .

Henry sat in front of an electric fire in Sarah's sitting room, wearing Sarah's bathrobe and brooding. When Sarah entered with two mugs of coffee he looked up gloomily. She smiled, gave him his coffee and kneeling by the fire started to brush her hair dry. Henry reached out and tugged it.

'Come and sit by me and tell me something,' he said.

Sarah pushed her hair off her face and turned to him.

'What?' she said smiling.

'How much of it really happened?'

'Oh dear,' said Sarah, 'if you really want to know. . .'

'I really want to know what *really* happened.'

'Well then,' said Sarah doubtfully, 'I'll tell you everything I know about it. But I think you'd better forget it all again tomorrow.'

'With pleasure,' said Henry shuddering. . .

For a man who had spent an extremely enjoyable and relaxing evening, Dr Lovell passed a surprisingly bad night, plagued with confused and uncomfortable dreams. He remembered when he woke at first light, that he had been standing on a hillside with a horde of other people, preparing for a battle or something. A little way off he saw Sarah Peach and his daughter Lucy of all people. There was a lot of scrambling around after that, and he could hear Sarah yelling, her red hair blowing in the wind like a banner. Well, the storm was real enough, he thought sleepily as he listened to the rain lashing across the window.

He lay awake for some time but eventually fell asleep again. He did not feel as if he had fallen asleep, but he must have, because he started dreaming once more. There was this large striped mouse sitting on the window sill, telling him how pleased it was to meet him at last, and talking about Heisenberg's work on a unified field theory, and explaining its difficulties about getting hold of up-to-date literature on the subject. The surprising thing was that the mouse had some very interesting and original things to say on this and one or two other matters, so that even though Dr Lovell *knew* that he was dreaming, and was chuckling all the time to himself over the whimsicality of his subconscious mind, he simply had to get out of bed to find a pencil and paper, and work out a few of the mouse's points with it. The dream was so real that he even found himself taking great care to move quietly so as not to wake his wife.

'She might wonder what was going on,' he explained to the mouse, who beamed at him understandingly and polished its spectacles with intense dedication. . .

'Shall I make some cocoa?' said Lucy.
'Might as well. Is there anything to eat?' said Martin. . .

Old Mr Lovell woke stiff and cold at daybreak, to find that he had fallen asleep in an armchair in his living room. He yawned and looked at the clock: after four o'clock. He heard his doorbell ring downstairs and remembered that it was that which had woken him. Who on earth. . . ? Still half asleep he stumbled down the stairs and opened the door, to find himself face to face with – himself! No, not quite himself. Himself a little older, perhaps.

'Well then young Joe?' said Captain Lovell grinning at him.

'Granddad!' exclaimed Mr Lovell. 'And Snowy too. You know I had a feeling that was his jug Bea found, and I was sure I'd seen him about lately, but I thought I must be going soft in my old age. Come in.'

'Thanks lad,' said the Captain. 'I was just passing, and I said to old Snowy here, "We can't pass Joe's door without looking in, can we?"'

As Mr Lovell led the way up to his flat he laughed out loud.

'You know, if I could always choose my dreams, I don't think I'd ask for better than this,' he said.

They sat down on opposite sides of the table in the living room and looked at each other, while Snowy sat in the armchair washing his face.

'How about a cup of tea?' said Grandfather Lovell.

'Just the job!' said Great-great-grandfather Lovell.

Lucy and Martin sat on Martin's bed in their pyjamas and dressing gowns, drinking their cocoa. Martin had the notebook in which he had recorded all their adventures, open on his knees.

'You're not going to write it all down now, are you?' Lucy said yawning tremendously.

'No, tomorrow will do. I'm just looking back,' Martin replied.

'It's tomorrow already,' said Lucy.

She too started to look back sleepily over the whole adventure, right back to the beginning in Aunt Bea's flat and the story Snowy had told them. *Hey diddle diddle, the cat and the Fiddler* – no that wasn't right, but it ought to be. . .

'I wonder what happened to Daisy?' she said.

'Who?' said Martin.

'You know, the cow that jumped over the moon that night.'

. . . The little dog laughed . . . and the dish ran away . . . there was something funny about the spoon though, thought Lucy, what was it?

'Oh yes,' said Martin vaguely, 'what I'd really like to know is what's happened to the Tokens.'

Lucy remembered what was wrong with the spoon. It was flat, that was it – 'Flat and leaf-shaped . . . not a lot of use for spooning' . . . long and thin with a flat pointed end. Like . . .

'I don't suppose we shall ever know,' said Martin shutting the book.

. . . Like a spear.

'They ran away,' said Lucy leaning back against the wall and closing her eyes.

'What?' said Martin. 'Who ran away?' He stared at her.

'The Tokens,' Lucy muttered. 'The dish ran away with the spoon. Only it wasn't a spoon, it was a spear. She was standing on top of them all the time. . .'

Her voice trailed away and the empty mug slipped out of her hand and rolled on to the floor. Martin shook her shoulder.

'Lucy! Lucy!'

But she was fast asleep and all he could get out of her was a little smile.